Knowing When to Leave

Knowing When to Leave

Kristina Neihouse

SeaStory Press
Key West, Florida

Knowing When to Leave
© 2018 by Kristina Neihouse

Author photo, page 195, By Tony Gregory
Cover photo by Edgardo Alvarado-Vázquez

ISBN 978-1-936818-46-4
LCCN 2018949247

SeaStory Press
1508 Seminary St. #2
Key West. Florida 33040
www.seastorypress.com

Acknowledgements

First I would like to thank Andy Kimball for his support, his advice, for everything he is.

Then to the first of my first readers, Lisa Mahoney, Chelsea Catherine and Andreea Mihalcea. They read early, rough drafts and said "Yes! Keep going!"

At the final stages they were joined by readers Carolyn Ferguson, Lori Kelly and Kristina Welburn to read an early completed draft and say "Well done! But…" They all found holes, typos and commas that I missed (or added.) And to Edgardo Alvarez-Valdez for the inspired cover that resulted from his own early reading of the text.

I owe extreme gratitude to the financial assistance provided in the form of a grant from the Anne McKee Artist Fund of the Florida Keys, Inc. But more importantly to me, they were the first organization to say "yes, we will support you" when I needed it most. Thank you Anne McKee.

Finally, thank you again to Andy, because it all begins and ends with you.

Author's Note

When I was almost finished with this book I read a poem about
planting a tree on the last day of the world,
and it made me pause.

Be prepared. Plant every day.

Prologue

Thursday July 28

I hadn't seen Becky in a couple of days, since we talked on the front porch that night. Naturally, she spends all her time with Evie so it's not like I'm being ignored. I'm at work most days anyway, if you can call it that. I go in everyday just to be around Mike. Pam is there too. It's like we don't know what else to do with ourselves.

When I heard Becky come in just before sunset, I was on the floor on the other side of my bed, reading. I didn't get up. Her door creaked as she pushed it halfway closed. A breeze blew in through the open windows, rooms and hallway. Later, the screen door slammed and Dad and TJ's voices drifted up. Since Gaston drastically reduced the livable portions of the island, they'd been riding bikes around at sunset, "seeing and being seen" is what Dad says, but it seems like they're on patrol.

A chair scraped across the wood floor. I'd been alone the entire afternoon and had no desire to be seen, so instead of going down, I moved to the top of the stairs to listen.

"I don't think anyone is paying attention to anything past First Avenue. Electricity, trash pickup, there's nothing going on," Dad said. "I rode around with one of the landscapers from the Hudson property. Some streets past Fifth aren't even passable because of downed trees, power lines or odd household items that floated out of destroyed houses."

TJ continued, "Most places out there are unlivable. With no power, the mold sets in. One of the guys I used to work with lived on Northside Drive. He only had six inches of water over his floors and considered himself lucky that it didn't get into the electrical outlets. But now the baseboards are swollen and turning green."

"Soon to be black mold," Dad added.

"Yep, he's taking his chances and heading north in a few days."

"Really."

I could hear the questioning in Dad's voice and pictured him leaning back to look at the stained glass lamp that hung over the table. That's how he thought, by looking up.

"What do you think about that?" he asked.

It was so quiet, I could hear TJ sigh. "I don't know, Robbie. I feel okay here. It's our home. I know what to expect. I know the people who are left. I know how to live here. But up there." I pictured TJ waving towards the north. "Between crazy newspaper stories and paranoid TV news out of Miami, you couldn't pay me to leave Key West right now. But what about you? What about Josie? What about all the girls?"

"I have to keep telling myself they'll be fine, that we'll all be fine. That I can take care of them, no matter what. I know I can do that here. From what I've heard, I might not be able to do that up there."

"We all have to take care," TJ said.

———

The connection cannot be seen. Seeva knows when Cloyal makes a discovery. No humans yet, but Cloyal has found something.

Seeva perches in a mangrove, waiting for the sun. Instead of watching it rise over the jagged skyline in the distance Seeva faces the open sea. The sky brightens, dark blue fading to light, clouds tinged with pink and orange. Out here, it's as it should be. Ocean and sky, changing colors from turquoise to blue to gray in no particular order. White herons and silver blue tarpon, flying, swimming and living amongst the mangroves. Some mornings calm and quiet, others blustery and chaotic. Often, as today, there is no time.

Cloyal found something.

Turning, Seeva sees the uneven horizon that borders the fragments of an area that used to be called Naples. As they make their way south, Cloyal checks signs having memorized names of areas they would pass through.

Diving, Seeva swims to Cloyal. Here, the sea is clear and clean. Later, as Seeva approaches what is left of the town, the mangroves thin and the water turns murky as the depth decreases. When travelling through vacant cities and towns it is safest to swim on the surface as long as possible. Though tough, the hidden debris of submerged streets could still cut the thick soles of Seeva's feet.

Seeva follows Cloyal's path, in and around new ecosystems formed in fallen trees, downed street lights, and toppled billboards and signs, eventually wading through ankle deep water to a cinderblock building, three stories high. Stairs run along the outside, all the doors and windows are gone. Anything moveable blew away years ago in the pummeling winds and caustic seas. Not many human structures survived the hurricane season and sea saturation of 2016. Most of the remaining buildings are concrete or metal frame and no more than four stories high. Taller buildings

3

collapsed in gales or from sitting in salt water for almost fifteen years. Wooden structures rotted away a decade ago.

Cloyal is in the last room on the second floor. Before turning into the open doorway, Seeva stops, inhales the soft, salty breeze, and admires the sun. The orange sphere now clear of the horizon on this rare, still morning.

Cloyal sits on the floor holding a notebook with a black and white cover, pages puffy with past damp. Seeva sees the blurry markings on the pages. Years ago Cloyal taught Seeva this form of human communication as they travelled to the Area Municipality.

Cloyal is the same compact size as Seeva, four feet tall with cool, honey colored skin that does not burn. As the others, they are right for this climate, with short hair just dark enough to protect their heads, and light hazel eyes flecked with black that are not bothered by the hot, bright sun. They both wear a pale linen sheath. From a distance they might resemble girls or young women. But they are neither.

"You need to see this," Cloyal says. *Key West, 2016.*

Year of Change, they both think. With shaky hands, Seeva takes the notebook. Before releasing it, Cloyal adds, *humans and O-meg together. Time for you to learn. I will continue the search.* Cloyal looks at Seeva, holds the hand that holds the notebook. *I will be back.*

Seeva, uneasy in a room alone, looks out the window. Birds fly and call, soar and dive, only the sun is visible, not the remnants of humans, broken buildings being reclaimed by the terrain. Humans are gone.

Seeva sits on the clammy linoleum and opens the notebook.

4

Friday January 1

Hello New Year, hello first journal. The journal assignment from English class was pretty fun so I decided to keep one on my own. I bought one of the thickest composition notebooks I could find, the ones with the black and white marble cover. I wanted Becky to do it too, but she's still bummed about Dave leaving Key West for the Latin American Front, like, five months ago. She's written him a lot of letters, on paper. Kind of retro, but, internet and cell phone coverage has been bad so it's really her only choice.

When they hooked up last spring, before Dave graduated, I told her not to date a guy who was joining the Reserves. According to Dad nobody's in reserve anymore, everyone's being sent south.

Now, half way through my senior year of high school, with no idea what to do next. Should I leave Key West? Should I stay? And do what? Or here's a thought, what if I try to find my mother? I don't know, at seventeen, how much do I need to know right now?

Anyway, I figured this was a good way to reflect, consider, prepare…for something? Maybe for my "adult" life to begin?

Saturday January 2

Becky helped dye my hair red, literally, tomato red. I wanted something different to start the year. After, we were kneeling on a towel on the tile floor by the tub. The last of the red dye had just swirled down the drain. She held out a mirror and we started to laugh.

"My mom would never let me do anything like this."

Her mom doesn't let her do much of anything, but Becky manages, better than me. She used to go out most weekends and tell her mom she was with me. And she used to see a lot of guys, until Dave. I don't know, it seemed like too much work, the guys, the schemes, dealing with her mother. Although I don't have much to compare it to, my mother left right after I started first grade.

When Dad saw my hair he shook his head. "I played with Mr. Potato Head when I was a kid. Now I have a Ms. Tomato Head for a daughter."

"Ha-ha," I said. He hugged me and kissed the side of my head. We're almost the same height, and it's not because he's short.

Monday January 4

At school everyone was crazy about my hair, but every time someone gushed about how awesome it looked or how cool it was, I wanted to scream. Maybe the red was <u>too</u> different. I hated all the attention. By lunch I wanted a hat. When I got home I washed it over and over with Dad's medicated dandruff shampoo. I wanted my hair back—plain and brown.

I lost count of how many times I washed it. The water was cold, my fingers were wrinkled and my scalp tingled when I finally got out of the shower, my own hair color back, mostly. I'll wear it in a bun tomorrow. Maybe Becky can cut it all off this weekend— that'll be different.

Dad didn't comment when he came in to check on me. I was in bed reading. He just kissed the top of my head as usual and patted the dogs, Sargent, black and white, and Pepper, grey and white, rescue mutts. I have a double bed so we all just fit.

"I'll buy you another bottle of shampoo," I said from behind my book.

"No worries, Josie. You're fine."

Maybe I'm trying too hard for something different.

Saturday January 9

Becky spent the night and cut my hair, like *really* short. I don't look like me. I love it.

Wednesday January 13

Not a lot going on. I guess I thought that by keeping a journal more would start happening?

Becky still hasn't heard from Dave. I remind her mail service probably isn't the best where he is. I wouldn't tell Becky this, but Dad has no confidence in the government, especially the Latin American Front. People around town think he's a bit of a conspiracy nut but how long have we been down there "protecting the country's interests"? That's how my fifth grade teacher taught us geography, by tracking American troops throughout that area. Anyway, Dad says it's not all about the oil anymore. He has a lot of theories. Maybe it's time to start asking him about some of them.

Friday January 15

Becky got a letter from Dave. She was all happy because he'd signed it "love, Dave." But that didn't last.

"So, where's the letter from?" I asked. We were on the bus home. Yes, we are seniors and we ride the bus. The new principal won't allow any student to drive their own car. (Not that Becky or I have a car—or even a driver's license. But it's the principle of the thing she says.)

"It was postmarked from Panama, like two months ago." She was looking out the window. I waited.

"Aaaaand, how's he doing?"

"It's bad down there," she said, still not looking at me.

"Bad?"

"You remember how excited he was before he left? He really believed he was doing the right thing, going to protect our interests in Latin America."

I could hear Dad saying our interests should remain in our own country, but I didn't say anything.

"In his letter he never mentioned that. He only wrote about the heat and the bugs. He also said nothing was clean."

"Clean? Like what?" She must be worried. I usually don't have to work this hard to get her to talk about a boyfriend. Also, she squints when she's upset, like she's trying to figure out what's happening, what exactly is upsetting her happiness. She's squinting now.

"That's all he said. 'Nothing is clean here.'" She used air quotes for the last part. Becky loves using air quotes.

Becky and I have known each other our whole lives, almost. We met at day care when we could hardly walk or talk. But we found each other. According to Carol, her mother's younger sister, we would both cry and cry when we were dropped off, until we saw each other. Now we say our opposites fit us together—my brown to her blonde, my lean to her curves, my calm to her flights, my quiet to her spirit.

I'm watching her closely with this Dave thing. I know how she can be, getting overly attached to a guy then moving on, often to just another guy. Dave's been gone for five months and I haven't heard about any other guys. This might actually be different.

Sunday January 17

So how weird is this? There was a TROPICAL STORM yesterday. It got a name and everything—Alex. It was quick—in the Straits, then north and out to sea. I thought it was a cold front, but according to Dad the wind and ocean currents were just right and a sub-tropical something formed and blah blah blah. The point is—seriously, it's **January**. Another big Happy 2016, our first ever twelve-month-long hurricane season??

Monday January 18

There was a newspaper from the mainland on the table when I came down for breakfast. (Later than usual—no school today—Martin Luther King, Jr. Day!) Dad had already left. He's a property manager for a bunch of different snowbirds (rich people who only come to Key West for a few months in the winter to escape the snow of their *other* homes). He also does odd jobs for people all around the island— *"from yards to roofs, from inside to out, from the bottom up"* is his motto. He has no real schedule.

An empty coffee cup sat on top of the folded paper, only the headline showed. Brown circles of dried coffee covered the rest so I couldn't read the article, which was fine. I would never tell

Dad, but usually I only read the headlines. He used to be a big believer in the "power of the press" until the Allied Media Group started buying it all. The television was the first to go when he discovered all the news channels were owned by Allied Media. And he used to work for the local newspaper, *The Key West News* until last year when it was bought by some big media company. Dad started digging and found out the company was owned by another company that was controlled by Allied Media, so he quit.

Anyway, here's the headline from *The South Florida Times*:

New Mosquito Borne Virus O-meg Spreading in Caribbean

Dad rarely gets the paper, especially from the mainland. He says there's nothing there that's news to him. Since leaving *The Key West News* he relies on public radio and his Ham radio for news. So the fact that there is any mainstream news source in the house is something to note.

Tuesday January 19

Super weird, another *South Florida Times* on the table this morning, headline above the fold:

Two Cases of the O-meg Virus Found in Miami-Dade

O-meg—that was the same word from yesterday's headline. Interesting, or at least more interesting than anything else going on right now.

———

Seeva lowers the notebook and leans back against the cool cinder block wall. It started early that year, 2016, the storms, the news of

O-meg.

By the end of that year, the country had shrunk, and humans retreated. Government and military reformed on the high plains and mountains in an area that used to be called Colorado. High, dry and cold, that's how humans feel safe now. The O-meg kept to the coasts, along the south, near the sea, near the sun.

The year is now 2029, or 13 PC (Post Change). From Cloyal and others in their Area, Seeva had learned some humans started a new count when the O-meg arrived, and the hurricanes rearranged the country.

Seeva is starting to see there is more to know about humans.

This Josie has much to share.

Saturday January 23

Tonight, I asked Dad about the O-meg thing when we had Sargent and Pepper out for their walk.

"Where did you hear about it?" He ran his hand through his hair, lighter and curlier than mine.

I didn't mention the papers left on the kitchen table. I told him I saw *The Key West News* headline this morning in the box on the corner.

Mosquito Control Keeps Eye on O-meg

"Wow," he said. "It made it above the fold." We'd stopped to let the dogs sniff and pee on a bush at the corner. Most corners now had decorative plants or small trees. Key West was getting very polished, and the greenery started off looking nice and tropical and photogenic. Then it faded after a few months of baking summer sun, windy winters and frequent visits from neighborhood dogs.

"Becky said she's heard it mentioned on the news. It's some kind of virus."

"You know I love Becky, but don't listen to anything she says second hand from the TV news. Even firsthand, since AMG stepped in, it's usually wrong or exaggerated."

"I know, but then I saw it on *The Key West News* front page this morning."

"Again," he laughed. "Usually wrong or exaggerated. Actually, in this case, more than likely wrong. Don't forget AMG owns them too."

He smiled. I love his smile, comforting but not forced. People say I have his smile. We'd stopped again. Sargent sniffed noses with another dog, a standard poodle. Dad nodded at the tall woman holding the leash, a neighbor from down the street.

"Seriously honey, don't worry." He put his arm over my shoulders as we walked away. "We'll be fine."

I knew that, but I also knew he wasn't telling me everything.

Tuesday January 26

Surprise surprise, Becky and her mom aren't talking again.

"When I got home yesterday there was no letter from Dave and I started crying," she told me on the bus this morning. "Then my mother came in sighing and trying to analyze me. I yelled at her—told her she didn't understand."

Not a good thing to say to Becky's Mom. She has a PhD in Psychology and teaches at the community college. You'd think it was a big private university the way she talks. Anyway, Becky came home with me from school. Dad was out back sweeping leaves off the deck and singing along with the stereo when we stepped out of the back door.

He stopped sweeping and sang to us, "won't you come out and play?"

"Hello ladies, I knew I'd see both of you," he said. "Saw Becky's mom in Publix and she started going on about your mood swings, Becky." He swept the leaves into a pile. "I told her Josie had invited Becky to stay over so you could study for the big geometry test tomorrow."

"We took geometry last year, Dad." I grabbed the yard waste bucket to help with the leaves.

"Whatever, I'm sure you two will find something to study."

Becky went over and hugged him. "You're the best Mr. McKenzie."

Becky had no father, I had no mother. My Dad filled both slots most days and I felt lucky. Between him, my uncle and Becky's aunt I guess we did okay. I try to not think about my own mother. Who knows maybe she would have been as controlling as Becky's, not that Becky was actually controllable.

Wednesday January 27

Becky bought the mainland paper while we waited for the bus this morning. A cold front had blown in, and the wind howled. It was freezing, probably in the fifties with the wind. I had my hands stuffed in the front pocket of my sweatshirt and the hood pulled up. It looked like she was reading the paper while we got on the bus and sat down. Then she waved the crumpled paper in my face, and started talking way fast.

"Oh my god, Becky stop!" I grabbed the paper from her. All I could make out was the headline:

O-meg Swamps Venezuela's Ailing Healthcare System

"That's where Dave is!"

"I thought he was in Panama?" I tried to smooth the paper in my lap.

"They were, in the beginning. But it's been like six months since he left so who knows where he is."

"Well, Venezuela is pretty far away, and there's a whole other country separating it from Panama."

"I know, I know," she said. "But they say the virus is spread by mosquitos and they don't exactly follow borders, Josie."

I put my hand on her shoulder.

"Breathe."

She inhaled.

"Okay," I continued. "In the last letter did he say anything about the troops moving?"

"Oh, you mean his last letter of all the letters I've received so far? His last letter was his first letter, and no, he didn't say anything about troops or where he was, only that 'nothing was clean.'"

"Let's not worry." I wanted to smile but she's been so moody lately I wasn't sure how she'd take it.

"Easy for you to say."

"Look, he's there with the military. They're watching out for the troops."

"Not according to your dad," she said.

True, I thought.

"Don't freak out, Becky," I said and smiled. "Until there is something to freak out about."

She huffed and sat back in the seat. I left the crumpled paper on the bus when we got to school.

Saturday, January 30

Becky called this morning. She'd gotten another letter from Dave yesterday, postmarked two weeks ago from Venezuela. The letter was on the kitchen table so her mother must have seen it. She was in no mood to deal with her, so she came over. She pretty much cried herself to sleep, saying something about doing things differently.

I read the letter while she slept. It didn't say much, just that he missed her and Key West. He wrote that he'd never really considered the island home since his Dad had transferred in with the Coast Guard during his junior year of high school. And with all the tourists and snowbirds it felt too transient. But then he met her. And now that he was so far away he realized what home could mean. The letter ended:

I love you. I'm ready to come home.

Home. Key West is my home, Becky's too. We live here, really live here, my Dad's family born and raised on this tiny rock off the coast of America—that's what my grandfather used to call it. Some, like Dave, or I guess my mother, arrived too late so they still looked for something out in the world or on the mainland to call home. I wonder sometimes what might be out there, whatever it was that pulled my mother away from the island, away from me.

Becky and I spent the afternoon on the front porch with the dogs. We talked about school and the possibility of college. It was in the low seventies. Becky and I wore leggings, socks and faded Pepe's sweatshirts. We both had mugs of tea.

"I don't know what I'm going to do after graduation but I doubt I'm going anywhere," Becky said. She looked up at me and smiled. "Don't tell my mother."

I tucked my toes under Pepper's warm belly. She gave a little doggy groan. "I know. My Dad can't afford college…plus since the government has screwed up the educational system, even a scholarship wouldn't help." What I didn't want to say was how much I'd been thinking of leaving after graduation, college or not.

Two guys walked by wearing shorts and t-shirts.

"They make me colder just looking at them." Becky sipped her tea. "They must be tourists. I hope they got a deal. Tropical storms, cold fronts, not exactly paradise weather."

I inhaled minty steam from my mug. "Anyway, my Dad says the government loan system is like the factory towns of the Depression. He calls it a vicious circle—once you get a college degree it takes you forever to pay off the loans, so you're always tied to the government in some way."

Pepper rolled over and I rubbed her spotted belly with my foot. "Plus, I've heard corporations look down on applicants who had to take out loans in the first place. So, the only people who get the high paying corporate jobs are those who never had to take out loans to begin with."

Becky laughed. "Josie, you sound like your Dad! You should totally write a paper about that for our Social Issues class. Burke would love it."

I shook my head. "Probably not, Dad had Burke for history, I'm sure he would see my Dad all over it." Sargent got up, stretched so the ridge of hair down his back stood up then turned around once and lay back down with a huff by Becky's chair.

"But, it's true," I said. "Remember when Stacy Peters tried to get into a university on the mainland last year? She said it wasn't worth the hassle of loans and then trying to get a good job. Now, she's taking classes at the community college and working full time at Publix."

Becky reached down and scratched Sargent behind his ears. "I think people say your Dad is a crazy conspiracy theorist because he's saying things no one wants to hear."

"Probably." A woman across the street was taking a picture of a chicken scratching the gravel in front of the library. Recently I found myself looking at tourists—wondering where they were from, why they wanted to come here, what I might find exotic in their home town.

Tuesday February 2

Another newspaper on the table this morning. Appropriately, it felt like Ground Hog day: same subject, different day. Today's headline from *The South Florida Times:*

Six New Travel Related Cases of O-meg Confirmed in Florida

So, I hadn't even heard of O-meg like two weeks ago. I guess it's going to be a big deal.

Thursday February 4

And again, today's headline from *The Key West News*:

Governor Declares O-meg Emergency

I found the paper on the coffee table when I got home from school. Scrawled across the article with a black Sharpie Dad had written, "Great!?!?! Gov't getting involved…" I sat on the couch, not sure if the message was for me or just his own doodle. Pepper jumped up waiting for her walk. Sargent stayed on the floor looking aloof.

I wondered if Dad left the newspaper around for my benefit. Like he wants me to know what's going on, or at least what the Allied Media Group says is going on.

When AMG took over the Internet a few months ago, Dad got rid of our computer. Even before that, the Internet connection was so slow you couldn't count on it. We still have computers at school, but now the Internet is on a schedule; Monday through Friday from seven in the morning til eight at night, according to Becky weekends are iffy. It felt weird at first but Dad assured me with AMG in control the information couldn't be trusted anyway.

Now we get our information old school: radio and newspapers. Dad has a whole room downstairs for all his radio equipment. Some of it he uses to try to contact other people around the country, sometimes farther than that. Plus the public radio stations. So, it's not like we're totally cut off.

The count goes up. Even Becky's paying attention. She's the one who showed me today's mainland paper as soon as she got on the bus.

The South Florida Times headline:

Surgeon General: 14 O-meg Cases in Florida All Travel Related

"What do you think about this?" she asked me. She put the paper between us on the seat and got a protein bar from her bag.

"I think you usually don't eat breakfast," I told her. "What's up?"

"I don't know, I feel hungry all the time, unless I'm barfing. I think this," she tapped the newspaper, "and Dave, and my mother are all getting to me."

I wanted to ask about the barfing, but she asked me if she could spend the weekend at my place. She didn't bring up the headline again, until dinner, when she showed the newspaper to my Dad.

She pushed spaghetti around on her plate, the big yellow one with a lopsided smile and two misshapen dots for eyes. For months after my mother left, Dad took me to the Paint a Pot shop on the corner of Eaton and Caroline every Saturday. We made one set of dishes each weekend, two different sized bowls and two plates. Each piece signed on the back with a J and D separated by a heart. Tonight Dad's plate had a thick peace sign over a rainbow background. Mine was a swirl of different shades of purple.

"So, what do you think, Mr. McKenzie?"

"I don't think you should worry about it," he said.

I smiled into my jar that served as a drinking glass. Exactly what I thought he'd say, but she pushed.

"Come on, it's everywhere," she said and put her fork down. She was serious, I could feel the vibration of her knee bouncing up and down under the table.

"What have you seen on TV?" he asked, spearing a tomato.

"It's about the same as the papers, I guess. It just sounds worse with all the raised voices and flashy pictures." She waved her hands around. "I try to not watch, that's why I like it here so much." She turned towards the living room area.

Basically, the entire first floor is one large room. The kitchen is along one wall and has an oversized wooden table made by one of Dad's artist friends. It kind of divides the space. On the other side of the stairs is Dad's radio room, and then the living room area is at the back. Except for the table, our furniture comes from the properties Dad manages for the rich snowbirds. Some of them redecorate every other year. There's an oval braided rug, a leather couch covered with old blankets because who has a leather couch in Key West? Anyway, the couch faces the back of the house with a wall of French doors that open onto the covered back porch and deck. Plus random recliners and upholstered chairs, coffee and end tables, all very nice if some might say a bit outdated. Sometimes I like to look at the place through other people's eyes. It is comfortable, a shabby comfort. Home.

"You're always welcome here. You're a part of the family," he told her.

Nice question dodge, Dad, I thought.

He looked at me. "I will take care of you girls. Don't worry." Then he really changed the subject and asked about an algebra test we had that week.

This morning when Becky and I came down to the kitchen Dad was just folding the local paper. He tossed it onto the table. The headline read:

Florida Readies for Fight with O-meg Virus

We waited for a comment but he just drank his coffee and stared at the table. I got out the granola and almond milk. When we sat at the table he started talking.

"Today I'm going to the nursery to get a couple of fruit trees, more containers and potting soil. I have some seeds left. I'm going to spend tomorrow expanding the garden."

"Umm, Dad the growing season started in November."

We had spent the weekend before Thanksgiving planting seeds for tomatoes, green beans, and all kinds of lettuce. It was a good weekend, getting our hands dirty, deep in the soil that Dad works hard to keep amongst the coral and rocky surface of his beloved island.

"I know, I know but it doesn't hurt to plant more."

"Sure, Dad." I looked at Becky, but she was reading the paper.

So he spent the day shopping. We spent the day lying around. It was overcast and drizzly but never really rained. I was reading *Gulliver's Travels* and Becky had picked up some kind of "woman's magazine" somewhere, but ended up spending most of the afternoon sleeping in one of the recliners with Sargent stretched out next to her.

I love living in a place where a cloudy, grey day is a pleasant change.

Becky must have gone to the corner box and gotten a paper super early. She woke me up, like, poked me in the ribs to wake me up.

"Josie, Josie, are you awake?" The sun wasn't up, what did she think? She went on before I could say anything. "O-meg is in the paper again. What plans do you think they're talking about? What can they do at this point?"

I rolled away from her. "Jeez, Becky. For real? I have no idea. Go ask my Dad."

Okay, maybe not my finest "best friend" moment. When I finally woke up, once the sun was really up, the other side of the bed was empty except for the paper open to the Keys Life section.

Plans in Place to Combat O-meg

I wasn't ready to deal, so I read the article. It turned out to be a "fluff piece" about design concepts using mosquito netting and planters that don't collect water where mosquitos can breed. I wanted to go back to bed, but there were dishes clanging downstairs and noise from the backyard. Dad had put an album on his stereo. I knew they knew I couldn't sleep through it all, so I got up.

The house was chilly. Before going downstairs, I put on leggings and socks. The thermostat read 62 degrees, but the kitchen was cozy—and a mess. Becky was making cookies, flour all over the table, a stick of butter melting by the sink. She stood at the table scooping dough onto a piece of tin foil. There were rows of cookies on the cooling racks. I gave her a hip bump as I grabbed two cookies and went outside to work with Dad.

The wind was cool from a passing cold front. But the sky was clear, one of those days when it felt like the sun soaked your skin instead of fried it. Dad usually enjoyed planting but he seemed stressed and distracted. He kept moving containers and grumbling about space. We got a lemon tree and a lime tree replanted in bigger pots. We planted tons more herbs—basil, parsley, oregano, and rosemary. And many tomato plants.

"It's a bit late," he said. "Using starters will help."

"Help with what?" I asked.

He was staring at the tomato plants staked up along the back fence. He pulled me to his side. "Oh, nothing. I think it's time you learned how to make my mother's sauce. We are living in her family's house, so the sauce vibe should be good."

"Sure." I leaned into him, feeling the dampness of his worn t-shirt. He felt warm and smelled like potting soil. The screen door slammed, and Becky brought out the last batch of cookies, warm from the oven, and glasses of cold soymilk. I wanted to tease her about being so domestic, but it all tasted so good. We sat in the sun on the back porch and ate in silence. Maybe my thought of leaving will stay just that—a thought.

Monday February 8

Okay, I usually wouldn't say this, but I think Dad has gone crazy. He spent the day tearing up our back porch and used the lumber pieces to make garden plots where the porch used to be. He was patting soil around an eggplant when I came out the back door.

"Soooo, what's up Dad?"

"Hey JJ," he said with a smile and wiped the hair off his sweaty forehead. "I was just finishing up."

"I can see that," I said reaching to scratch behind the ears of the skinny black cat rubbing my leg. I never knew which one, Stanley or Prince until I touched him. Stanley would purr, Prince would hiss. This cat pushed into my hand and purred.

"Hello, Stanley."

"You know I was never a fan of the large porch, your mother wanted it. I think this is a much more practical use of the space. What do you think?"

"It's cool. We'll have lots of vegetables." I didn't know what else to say. He'd left the covered deck space outside the back door. Another one of the neighborhood stray cats rolled in the dirt, this one a small grey tabby. "And Niblet likes it."

"That's the idea," he said, rubbing the cat's belly. She hopped up and scampered away.

Later, when he was making dinner, I noticed something new taped to the fridge—a list of fruit trees in the neighborhood.

- Mango tree on Applerouth Lane
- Bread Fruit Tree on lane off of William by waterfront
- Fig Palm on the corner of Windsor by cemetery
- Blood Orange tree on White Street between Southard and Angela Streets
- Huge avocado tree on Roberts Lane off Frances Street by cemetery

There was also a map of Old Town, like the one they give to tourists. It had markings and notes indicating the trees.

Before I went to bed I heard him on the phone talking to his brother TJ, short for Tio Joe. I'm named after him, Josephine for Joseph. I love TJ otherwise I'd hate my name. But Josie isn't bad, or when Dad calls me JJ—for Joe Junior.

Anyway, it sounded like they were talking about water. TJ lives in their childhood home with a well and an active cistern. We have a cistern, too. Dad wanted to hook it up to rain barrels or something. He talked loudly so he must have been on his cell phone, even three blocks away reception has been bad.

Seeva is unsure what to make of this human, Josie's Dad. He seemed to understand, things were beginning to change in 2016. With the additional food he grew, with the rain barrels and cistern, he was preparing, even though the full extent of the impending changes was unknown.

Seeva wonders what is in store for this small human family on an island off the coast of a shifting world.

Thursday February 11

So a month ago I wonder how many people had even heard of O-meg? And now this headline from *The South Florida Times:*

18 O-meg cases in Florida, All Acquired Outside the U.S.

I guess that's a good thing? That the virus was acquired outside the US? I'm not sure what to think. Becky's been moody lately so I won't be asking her. And after the porch/garden thing Dad has seemed distracted. Also, February usually is his busiest month when most of the property owners come down to spend a month in paradise. He says Key West used be full of millionaires who came for the season. Now, it's billionaires who only come down for a month.

Friday February 12

But wait, there's more! From today's *South Florida Times:*

O-meg can be Transmitted by Sex, CDC Says as Virus Infections Rise in Florida

I could write something snarky about my sex life, but considering there isn't one the humor would be wasted. Guys don't notice me. It's not like I notice them either. As far as that goes, I live vicariously through Becky, or I used to, before Dave.

I would've joked with her about the sex headline, but she was quiet this morning. She looked tired and pale. She's usually very particular about make-up, but I could see the dark skin under her eyes.

Saturday February 13

I don't know why I wrote that about guys. I really don't care if they notice me or not—I never have. I've said it before—it just seems like too much work. Right now, this is what I'm noticing.

Headline from *The Key West News:*

O-meg Cases Reported In Florida Up to 20

I know it might not sound like a lot, but two weeks ago there were only six, so that's like more than a triple increase? Shit, I'm using math to read the newspaper, and Spring Break is still a month away? I need a break *now*.

Sunday February 14

I didn't see much of Becky over the weekend. She said she felt run down and planned to take vitamins and sleep. I'm sure the whole Valentine's Day thing didn't' help. Last year, Dave went all out, flowers delivered to the school, a super nice dinner compete with a limo ride. I guess that would be pretty sad to think back on.

Monday February 15

No school, President's Day. Although Dad says there's nothing to celebrate about this President, an evangelical TV preacher, who's trying to turn the country into his congregation. We call him Pastor Prez. He's running for re-election and there are rumblings our governor, Suarez, wants to run, but they are in the same screwed up party, so Dad doesn't think it would make much of a difference. The campaigning has begun, this will be my first election in November. There's an adult ritual for me!

I took the dogs on a long walk down to Higgs Beach and White Street Pier this afternoon. As I walked by Salute's restaurant I heard two wait staff discussing O-meg. It was on the front page of today's *South Florida Times again*:

New O-meg Infection in Broward Brings Florida Cases to 21

The guy pointed to a paper left on a table. "Wonder if this is why it's been so slow?"

The woman looked at the paper as she rolled silverware in a

napkin. "Don't know, but I'm ready to head North, virus or not. If the tourists aren't coming here, I need to go where they are."

This season has been slower than normal. Not that I'm complaining. Living so close to Duval Street we used to wake up to find beer bottles or Fat Tuesday cups littering the front yard all the time. I don't think that's happened at all this season.

Wednesday February 17

The Key West News, left on the kitchen table this morning:

Mosquito Control Targets O-meg Virus

Scrawled across the article: TOO LATE, BUBBAS.

I'm getting tired of this. I asked Dad about it at dinner.

"So, what do YOU think is up with this O-meg thing?" He stopped eating, the fork half way to his open mouth, buck wheat noodles dangling.

"Nice look. Come on, Dad, talk to me."

He smiled, a grin he used when he knew I was getting upset. As usual, I couldn't help but smile back.

"Come on, I'm almost eighteen." I put my spoon back in the bowl of miso broth and looked him in the eyes, the same brown as mine.

"You know I'll take care of you," he said.

"Of course. But, I don't need as much care as I used to."

"I can see that." His smile was gone.

"Anything from the radio?"

"Haven't heard much. I'm trying to get a radio contact somewhere in Latin America or the Caribbean." He twirled more noodles around his fork. "I don't think anyone really knows what's going on. I think AMG is trying to keep the hysteria and questions going."

He took a drink of water. "It's hard to get information, especially information AMG doesn't want to get out."

"Not surprising," I said and smiled. "But I know you'll take care of me."

I got up and kissed the top of his head, noticing gray scattered through the soft brown curls.

"And I'll take care of you too."

"Good to know. It's your turn to clean up from dinner."

He stood and ran his hand over my head. We have the same hair but it's hard to tell with mine being so short now. People say I look more like my Dad, which I guess is good so he doesn't have a reminder to look at every day. But I got an A in biology class so I know there are resemblances to my mother somewhere, whether he wants to see them or not.

———

Seeva stops reading. Allied Media always thought it was in control but didn't know what it was trying to control. Or that it was too late.

So much information.

Standing, one can see the ocean out of the open doorway. The sea in the distance is still calm, blurry with small waves. Turning, Seeva notices a fluttering through another door frame on the other side of the room, a thin light colored cloth covers the space. Pushing it aside, Seeva enters another room. Pieces of cloth are tacked over the open windows facing east. They move in the slight breeze. A long warped counter divides the larger space. On the counter next to an old refrigerator with no door are cans of various sizes in distinct piles.

In the corner near one of the windows is a dark green plastic chair and two plastic tables, on one there is a heavy plastic container. This, Seeva knows, is where Cloyal found the notebook. There are more books, some stacked on the other table, some laying open along the counter. An uneven stack of loose papers covered with writing fills a plastic bin on the floor, writing utensils on top.

It looks like a home, an attempt to make the space comfortable.

Seeva wonders how long it has been empty.

Thursday February 18

Becky showed me *The South Florida Times* as soon as she got on the bus this morning:

Two New O-meg Cases Confirmed in Miami-Dade; Statewide Infections at 24

"That's easy math," she pointed out. "A quadruple increase in only three weeks."

"In other words—a lot," I replied. I didn't realize she was keeping track.

Friday February 19

The count, and hysteria keep going up:

Steps Being Taken to Protect the Blood Supply from O-meg 26 Cases Statewide

This one sounded pretty creepy. I asked Dad about it at dinner. Just us this weekend—Becky's still being quiet and reclusive.

"And do not tell me not to worry," I told him before he even opened his mouth. He smiled.

"I wasn't going to say that. I'm sure they have some way to test donated blood at this point. If you or I wind up in a situation where we need a blood transfusion we'll have bigger things to worry about."

I narrowed my eyes at him.

"Seriously, Josie. It's just Allied Media trying to get everyone in a panic so when they develop a vaccine they can sell it for more money."

"Okay," I nodded. "That's more like it."

He laughed and bit into his cheese quesadilla.

"On a lighter note, why don't you get a job?"

I put down my spoon full of guacamole. "Why, am I eating too much? Using too much water?"

"Ha ha," he said. "I just thought it might give you something to do. I don't want you getting all caught up in this crap Allied Media is putting out. It's not like you need a lot of time to study, Miss Brainiac. You're sailing through your last semester of school."

I shrugged. "You think I should try one of the large chain stores in New Town?"

"Why not Gil's Groceries, right down the street. Locally owned. Close to home."

"Sure, I'll check it out tomorrow." I put the guacamole on my plate.

"I'll go with you. I've known Gil for years. He used to be

the track coach."

"Um, no offense..." I picked up a triangle of quesadilla and shook my head. "This might be my first job but even I know having Daddy come along would not look good."

He pushed away from the table with his empty plate. "See, I knew you were smart."

The plate was chipped so I knew it was the one with a clumsy palm tree on the front. I saw a flash of green and smiled, picturing our initials with the heart painted on the bottom.

Saturday February 20

I filled out an application and talked to Mike, the manager of Gil's Groceries, this morning. I've noticed him around the store since the beginning of last summer. He's Gil's nephew and doesn't look that much older than me. Anyway, he seemed nice, and kind of cute, I guess. He's taller than me and tan, with kind of shaggy dark blonde hair. I thought the hair made him look a little lost, like a California surfer boy stuck in Key West where there is no surf.

"We go easy scheduling the high school kids, keeping in mind homework and such. If you need a certain night off for studying, or a party, just ask. And I won't schedule you for both Saturday and Sunday in one weekend."

"That's not a problem," I replied. "I don't go out."

He looked at me. I couldn't look away from his light blue eyes. (I don't t know why I wrote that.)

"Well, let's just start with a few hours to see how you like it."

I start next Friday. He'd already done the schedule for the

week so I'll just be watching the cashiers and bagging. I have to admit that I'm looking forward to it. I wonder if he'll be working that day.

Wednesday February 24

Becky stayed home from school today. She never stays home from school. With her mother's crazy schedule she says it's more relaxing to be at school. When she called me on the land-line before I left to catch the bus, her voice was thick and hoarse.

"You sound tired," I said.

"I feel tired. But at least I haven't barfed today."

"Yay."

"My mother's going to be at the college all day for midterms. I thought I would take advantage of having the house to myself and sleep."

While I waited for the bus I read the headline in the newspaper box on the corner.

Three Pregnant Women in Florida Test Positive for O-meg Virus

I wondered what that would mean for the babies, not that I have anything to worry about, now—if ever.

Friday February 26

Started work at Gil's this afternoon, I hung out at one of the registers, bagging and watching the cashier. There are only three registers plus one in the front of the office in a large open space that faces into the store. While bagging, I could see Mike moving around, coming in and out of the office to run the smaller register. I've shopped there for years but never knew all that went on—cash sales, credit cards, debit cards, wholesale restaurant accounts. There's also a deli and meat department in the back. There's a lot happening!

Tomorrow I'm going to help Pam fill delivery orders so I get to know where things are around the store. I have a pretty good idea but Pam's cool, a thin older lady with very blonde hair, very tan skin and a very raspy voice. Between customers she told me she's worked there "forever." And laughed until she coughed. From the office I heard Mike say "be nice Pam, don't scare away the new employee."

"Don't worry, she looks tough," she said and winked at me.

Before I left, Mike showed me how to sign in and out for my shift on a computer in the office. Usually I picked that kind of stuff up easily but he had to show me twice. Maybe I was distracted, he smelled nice, like some kind of musky soap.

So that was my day—fun, and something different. A cold front had blown through last night. It was sunny today but didn't even hit 70 degrees. Once the sun went down it got cold. The thermostat outside the kitchen window is just under 60. I don't mind. I love hearing the wind in the palm trees and the chimes on the porch, putting on a sweatshirt and sleeping with socks on. Winter in Key West, I do love it.

But can't forget this, from *The South Florida Times:*

37 cases.

Work was super fun. Pam is a riot—weathered would be a good description for her. When she jokes about working there "forever," she's not far off. I think she's older than Gil but I wouldn't ask.

"I'm not even sure who hired her," Gil joked when he stopped in the cereal aisle to say hi. "I came in one morning and there she was behind a register ringing up an order to be delivered to The Chart Room."

"And you've been thankful every day since." She pushed the shopping cart to the tea at the end of the aisle. We both followed.

"You bet," Gil smiled at me. "You tell Robbie he raised a very nice young lady."

Mike was walking by. I blushed.

Sunday February 28

I hardly talked to Becky all weekend. When I finally got a hold of her tonight by text she replied like an hour later,

Can't talk, 2 tired, dr. appt. 2morrow

She used to get distant like this whenever she had a new boyfriend. Am I missing something?

Monday February 29

This morning on the bus I told Becky we should get the day off as a holiday since it only comes every four years. I could see her reflection as she stared out the window. The skin under her eyes was a heavy purple against her pale cheeks.

"You know, Leap year, February 29th?"

She held today's mainland paper in her lap.

Five More O-meg Cases Confirmed in Florida, Including Another Pregnant Woman

Before we got off the bus she finally looked at me.

"Sorry," she said. "I'm just distracted, worried about the English test this afternoon."

Becky never worried about English.

"We don't have a test this afternoon. You have a doctor's appointment."

"See," she said, and tried to smile. "Distracted!"

I walked slowly off the bus and let her get ahead of me. She didn't notice.

Tuesday March 1

Becky's pregnant. Almost four months pregnant. She hasn't seen Dave since the middle of summer, almost eight months ago.

She didn't come to school til after lunch. Then she told me on the bus ride home, like four blocks before her stop. She asked me to text her later. There's no cell service tonight. (Thanks Allied Media!)

Wednesday March 2

Becky and I didn't say much on the bus this morning. When we got to school she turned to me. "I cannot have you mad at me, Josie. Not now."

Not wanting to look at her, I zipped and unzipped the

small pocket on my backpack. "I'm not mad," I told her. "I just… don't know what to think."

She pressed the bridge of her nose. Her eyes must be tired from her nervous squint habit. "I don't either," she said, almost whispering. "But I need to talk to someone and you're the only one I have. You're the only one I want to talk to."

We agreed to meet at lunch when we'd have time and privacy. Am I surprised she slept with a guy other than Dave? I guess not. Am I surprised she never told me about it? Yes.

In the lunch room we found a table in the corner. The clacking trays and loud laughter meant we wouldn't be overheard. I barely sat down before she stared talking.

"So it was just some guy at a party. After homecoming last November, I was hanging out with Sasha. Remember her? We hung out a lot on weekends before I got serious with Dave." She took a breath and twisted the stem off her apple then put it back down on the table.

Becky talked a lot when nervous. Of course I knew Sasha. Becky tried to get us all to hang out together one Saturday night about a month before she met Dave. Wandering up and down lower Duval in front of the bars was not my idea of fun. Apparently, she told Becky I was too mopey. Becky stopped hanging out with her soon after that.

"I don't know," Becky continued. "I was missing Dave, thinking about last homecoming. That was when I first noticed him. He sat near me during the game." Someone sat at the next table. Becky lowered her voice. "Anyway, Sasha met this guy in the concession line who was having a party at his house. An hour later I was sitting on the couch thinking I should just go home when this cute guy sat next to me."

I'd heard many stories like this, but it'd been a while.

"He had really dark hair and this smooth skin. And an accent I thought sounded so sexy at the time. He was an exchange student."

"From where?" I asked.

She paused. "I don't know, he sounded Spanish, you know, Hispanic. I swear it was just that one guy, just that one time. Dave is different. He's not like…"

I put my hand near hers on the table. "I'm not judging you, Becky, I'm asking where the guy was from."

"I don't remember. I guess somewhere in Latin America." She didn't look at me. "I still have to tell my mother."

She started crying. I wasn't going to ask her anything else.

———

An O-meg in Key West, in 2016, maybe still?

Now Seeva feels what Cloyal has felt as they travelled south, the reason Cloyal chose this path. A tug, a pull. Why Cloyal wanted to go on this quest.

When the Elder of their Area called them all together and told of the next Sea Saturation foretold over the next twenty moons, Cloyal knew what that meant. The sea would rise again, and others still needed help. Cloyal was one of the first to volunteer. Seeva, lost before Cloyal, never questioned, just got ready to go wherever Cloyal would go.

Could this one, this early O-meg still be there? Would one know they were coming?

Seeva continues to read.

Thursday March 3

I smelled the Bustello from the top of the stairs. By the time I made it to the kitchen Dad's small white cup sat in front of him on the table, empty. At the stove I turned on the burner under the kettle and got a bag of green tea from the cupboard. He started teasing me a few months ago that if I was old enough for morning caffeine, I was old enough for Cuban coffee. Every time I smelled it I knew I wasn't that old yet.

"What's up this morning?" I asked.

"Look, the suits are getting involved." He turned the mainland paper so I could read the headline:

Business Round Table:
CEOs Express Concern but Not Panic Over O-meg

"Don't you feel safer already?" he asked.

Shaking my head, I poured hot water in my mug. It was kind of nice, a bit of normalcy at home. Or what passed for normal now.

Friday March 4

"Still nothing about Monroe County or Key West." Becky handed me the paper as soon as she got on the bus.

22 Cases in Miami-Dade County Alone

"In all these articles have you ever seen anything about the testing? Like when? Or where?" she asked.

"I thought you were reading the articles?"

I looked at her and we laughed. There she was—Becky, she had her hair down today, the blonde flowed around her face. Maybe a bit plumper, but laughing, and not so pale.

"I'm talking to my mother tonight," she said. And we stopped smiling.

"Let me know what you need. Anything, anytime. If you can't call just come over."

She smiled again. "I know."

Saturday March 5

Becky spent last night with us. As she put it, her mother was "not pleased." She didn't go into details.

She also told my Dad. We sat on the couch. I held her hand. When he noticed her squinting he pulled a chair over and sat in front of us. She spoke quickly—the guy was from somewhere in Latin America, an exchange student, gone now.

"My mom says I should get rid of...she said 'it.'"

I squeezed her hand.

"Do you know what you're having?" Dad asked.

She let go of my hand and jumped up. "A baby!" she yelled. Then wrapped her arms around her waist. "Just a baby."

Dad stood and hugged her. "I know, darling," he said. "I know. I was wondering if you knew the gender of the baby."

At that point Becky started to sob. I stayed on the couch while my Dad held her. She had her hands over her face. I saw her nodding, but she didn't answer.

Later, Becky and I stayed up talking. Another front blew

through yesterday, my window was open to the cool breeze. Under two of my grandmother's quilts piled on the bed, we talked about growing up, running around Old Town the summer before my mother left. We were six. Dad was helping a guy build a porch two blocks away from the Southern Gas propane office where my mother worked with Becky's Aunt Carol. The town used to be so quiet during the hot summers. Becky and I rode our tiny bikes up and down the street in front of the house where Dad was working. We didn't realize we were sweating until it ran down the side of our faces or the back of our necks. Dad didn't let us cross the intersections alone on our bikes so we left them and run to my mother's office. She gave us money to get something to drink from Dennis Pharmacy.

"Get juice, no soda," Carol called as we ran out. We loved ginger ale in those little green glass bottles with the screw top. After paying the cashier, we sat and spun around on the stools at the counter until one of the waitresses made us stop before we threw up.

"So much has changed," Becky said.

"Yeah, Dennis Pharmacy is now a bank," I said. A gust of wind hit the bamboo chimes, hollow notes mixed with sounds of the rustling leaves. "I wonder if this'll be the last front til next winter."

I thought she'd fallen asleep, then I heard her say, "by then everything will be different."

Monday March 7

South Florida Times: **50 Cases Statewide.** I wonder if Becky would count as a "case" now. Ugh, that's an awful thought.

Dad and I left the house at the same time this morning. He was laughing as he showed me the headline of *The Key West News:*

Mosquito Director Travels to Brazil Over O-meg

"I went to school with Miller," he pointed at the headline. "He's a complete germ-a-phobe. I'm sure when he ran for that office he figured it would be a desk job. I can just see him getting off the plane in one of those bright yellow hazmat suits." He tucked the paper under his arm as he walked away, still laughing.

Thursday March 10

Becky looked tired this morning. Before the final bell for homeroom she pulled me into the bathroom and pushed open all the stall doors to make sure we were alone. Then we went into the handicap stall.

"My mom totally went off last night," she started. "I guess the shock wore off. She yelled and called me names, even something about me being an incubator."

She leaned against the long low sink. I dropped my backpack and slid down the wall until I sat on the cool tile floor.

"Shit, Becky, I'm sorry."

She shrugged and tore off a square of toilet paper, folding it in half again and again until it was the size of a pea.

"I blocked her out at that point."

"You could've come over."

"I know, I know." She tossed the tiny wad of paper into the next stall. She rubbed her belly over the loose dress she wore. "But I still have to live there. I mean, I was never sure what I wanted to do after graduation, but now I know I won't be going anywhere."

She carefully pulled off another square of toilet paper.

"Have you...considered your options?" I asked, not looking at her. She needed to know I was there, with her, no matter what.

"Yes, that was the first thing my mother asked about."

"Sorry, just trying to cover all the best-friend bases."

"I know, J. It's okay." She looked down at the toilet paper in her hand. "By the time I went to the doctor I figured I was just past 16 weeks. Or into my second trimester, the doc said. In other words, anything other than carrying the baby would have to be done on the mainland. You know how hard Pastor Prez has made it."

She threw the tiny wad of toilet paper against the wall. "Which is fine. I hate making decisions," she shrugged. "So now the question is, what to do when she's born."

My butt was falling asleep on the cold floor. I stood and looked at her.

"Yep, a girl."

I smiled. "A girl."

"Of course my mother is still referring to her as it. Until I have the baby tested, she says she'll continue."

"Is there a test?"

"Apparently one of the professors at the college knows someone who knows someone at the University of Miami who can test unborn babies for O-meg. You know since the father is from

Latin America it gives my mother one more thing to freak out about."

She turned to look in the mirror over the sink, and pulled her hair out of its bun.

"Anyway, according to that guy in Miami if either parent has the virus it goes to the baby. And the babies in Latin America have not been pretty. Of course no one knows anything specific."

She finger combed her hair then put it back in a ponytail high on her head. "Guess I should have read those articles that referred to pregnant women with O-meg."

"I could ask my Dad. He's been trying to stay in contact with people throughout Latin America on his radio."

She shrugged and picked up my backpack from the floor. "Thing is, I feel fine. You know other than when I'm with my mother, I feel healthy and almost…happy. Shit, do not ask me why. I know I shouldn't be, I'm eighteen and pregnant."

"I know I don't have to tell you this Becky, but don't go to Miami. Don't leave the island. My Dad would fight for you as much as for me. Until we know more about this 'virus' you're safer here."

"I know," she held my backpack to her stomach and rested her cheek on top. The bell rang.

"Shit, what's the point?"

"Come on. It's Ramsey for first period today, you know she'll call your mother just for spite if you don't show up."

Becky handed me my backpack.

"And another thing I shouldn't have to tell you," I said. "There will be no gender stereotyping. No pink!"

She sighed and nudged me in the waist as we walked out

into the hall. "Thanks for keeping everything relative, Auntie J."

I liked the sound of that.

At those words Seeva stops-*girl, she, gender.* O-meg are female but these words are not used. The words of figurative boxes humans used to label and separate, *them* and *us.* To each other O-meg are *one.*

A seagull flies past the open window frame. Seeva stands to see it dive and pluck a fish from the water's surface that ripples between two collapsed metal structures that now shelter mangroves. Seeva longs to follow, dive and swim, out of the gray water of this place into the blue, into cool freedom. But one knows to continue reading, to learn more of that time, of the possibility of humans and O-meg living together.

Friday March 11

I went into the bathroom before Algebra and Sasha was there talking to a group of girls, all dressed in varying shades and styles of black. When they saw me, they stopped talking and left.

Whatever.

Monday March 14

Nice, un-dramatic weekend…and then we went back to school. People have started to stare at Becky. Even the teachers. It's not like she even looks pregnant, maybe a bit rounder but she's been wearing loose sundresses.

On a good note Becky had lunch with her Aunt Carol yesterday. She's pretty cool. Not surprising Carol was completely supportive of Becky, no matter what the outcome.

Tuesday March 15

"Watch your back out there today, Josie."

Dad gave me his annual Ides of March warning as I left the house. I should have passed it on to Becky.

Sasha must've figured out that Becky is pregnant. She was with her the night of Homecoming, and she can do enough math—the quiet Becky, the loose clothes—and remembers where the guy was from. Sasha is not one to keep things to herself. So today whenever Becky walked down the hall, kids moved to either side to get as far away from her as possible. In history, Mr. Burke held her paper at the very edge of the corner when he handed it back to her. Really? Kind of stupid. So we ignored them ignoring us.

I wanted Becky to come over tonight, but she decided to head home.

"My mother's not talking to me either, so it won't be that different from school," she gave me a half smile.

Three days until Spring Break. Cannot wait.

Wednesday March 16

After a rousing day of whispers and stares at school, Becky and I spent the afternoon in my backyard picking every ripe tomato there was and a bunch of herbs. Then I dug out my grandmother's tomato sauce recipe. It's written on a yellowed piece of loose leaf paper, and kept in a plastic sheet cover but still shows stains and pencil markings in her hand.

We chopped and boiled, seasoned and spiced, then simmered. While the sauce cooked we rode our bikes to the White Street Pier, the dogs running alongside. Becky was quiet, didn't say anything about what was happening at school. I didn't bring it up.

At the pier we threw a tennis ball for the dogs and watched the sky change as the sun set. Some guys fishing, and an older couple with a small dog that yapped at Sargent whenever he ran by with the ball were the only other people there. There were no tourists, no spring breakers. It might have been the middle of July except for the 6:30 sunset and 75 degree weather.

When we got home Dad had made the pasta and a salad. "Lettuce and a few tomatoes you missed from the garden," he told us. "Eat off the land, that's the idea."

A quiet meal, light chatter about school (assignments and classes NOT about the people.) He drove Becky home after dinner. She said she was trying to get along with her mother as much as possible, but they still just ignored each other. Between attitudes at school plus at home it seems like too much for her.

Friday March 18

HELLO SPRING BREAK!

Trying to keep busy so I picked up a bunch of shifts at Gils'. Mike went up to see his mom in Naples. And, Becky is still in constant battle with her mother, either verbal or the silent treatment, so she'll be staying with us for the whole week! She left her mother a note on the fridge.

Pretty uneventful week, until today. Becky decided to keep the baby. She went to talk to her mother yesterday, then came right back. I asked how it went.

"Typical," she said. I didn't ask anything else.

I wish Becky would live with us. The house can feel empty with just Dad and me. When Becky was here the other night and it started to rain, my Dad got her tea, a blanket, turned down the ceiling fan. I was next to her on the couch, my bare feet propped on the coffee table.

"Geez, Dad. Are you going to rub her feet too?"

He looked at her. "Do they hurt?"

She laughed. "No, no Mr. McKenzie," she said. "I'm fine." She blew on her tea and smirked at me when he went back to the kitchen. "Would you like a sip?'

I rolled my eyes. But it was kind of sweet. Becky's baby seems to have given him hope. He hasn't mentioned O-meg, AMG, the Latin American Front, and I haven't seen a newspaper in the house for a couple of weeks.

Sunday March 27

Dad went to talk to Becky's mother this afternoon. When he came back he looked confused. Becky and I were at the kitchen table working the Sunday crossword. He went to the sink and got a glass of water.

"She turned me away at the door, saying she would be more comfortable meeting in a neutral space. She suggested her office at the college. I pointed out that space wasn't so 'neutral' for me." He used air quotes. I asked if he'd done that with Becky's mother and he grinned. Becky coughed with laughter.

"Oh my god, I can just see her face—how she used to scowl at me when I did that."

He sat at the table and rubbed the wood with his thumb. "Becky, you're eighteen so ultimately the decision is yours. You know you're more than welcome to stay here as long as you like, even permanently. It's fine with us. But I'm still going to talk to your mother."

"It's your time," she said. "What's a four letter word that means contend?"

"We're meeting on Wednesday." He tapped the paper, "three down is wrong, should be expert."

He didn't mention what neutral space they decided on.

Wednesday March 30

There was cell service for like a minute this afternoon, Dad texted:

BRING BECKY HOME

He likes to text in all caps—says it's easier for him to see.

So Becky and I spent the evening getting her settled in the room across the hall that used to be a guest/playroom. Becky sat on the bed trying to organize her clothes that she'd brought in garbage bags from her house. Sargent had taken up residence at the foot of her bed.

Checking the closet, I found a box on the floor. When I bent to pick it up a spicy smell hit me from between the folded flaps. I had to sit down from the familiar scent. The box was full of my mother's old books. They smelled like her, like the sandalwood oil she used to wear. I remembered how she used to leave books lying around the house—on the kitchen table, on the couch, on the back porch chairs. I never knew the titles, but now I recognized the covers—*The Purpose Driven Life, Adventures for Your Soul, How to Love Yourself (And Sometimes Other People)*. As I closed the box, Dad came in.

"Wow, I forgot about those. Sorry, let me get that," he said, picking up the box. "I meant to take these to the library years ago."

I didn't say anything. Pepper's nails clicked out in the hallway. She came in and lay down next to me. I scratched the top of her head and she sighed. Becky came and stood next to me. I looked at the little blue butterfly tattooed on her ankle. One wing slightly larger than the other, courtesy of a one-time boyfriend from a couple years ago. When her mother saw the tattoo she almost had the guy arrested, a military kid who wanted to be a tattoo artist. The father was reassigned and the family left town soon after.

"Neither one of us has had the best mother role model," she said.

"Not really," I agreed.

"I want to do better, I really do."

Looking at the empty spot where the box had been, I wondered if everything could be okay. Maybe down here at the end of the road we would be all right.

———

So much was unknown at that time.

Seeva stands and walks outside. Not wanting to be surrounded by walls, one goes down the stairs, sets feet in the briny, murky water covering the last two steps. Looking out at what is left of the submerged street recognizable only by the path of gray opaque water it leaves between disintegrating and hollow buildings, rimmed by fallen power poles, dangling lines, and rusting automobiles. All slowly being broken down and absorbed into the sea, as nature returns.

Thoughts come of a new O-meg beginning with humans in 2016, wondering how it would be in Josie and Becky's home with the father.

Seeva knows how it can be. One breathes in the warm, salty air, smelling the sea. Outside, even amongst the ruins of humans, Seeva feels better, returns to the room and continues to read.

Friday April 1

News from around the state is back! According to *The South Florida Times*: **3 new cases.** Okay, I've lost track, Miami-Dade County? The entire state? I didn't even skim the article to find out. Does it even matter? It does make it hard on Becky. No one at school spoke to her all week. I even saw a cafeteria worker put on gloves before throwing her used tray and dishes in the garbage. And, she told me the principal sent a note to final period that he wanted to see her. She ignored it.

Sunday April 3

Pretty mellow weekend. Yesterday Becky and I dragged my grandmother's old manual sewing machine out of Dad's radio room and stuck it in a corner of the front room.

"I'm going to teach myself how to sew,' she declared.

It's like all the energy she used to put into guys has a new outlet—herself and her baby.

I worked today, so did Mike. I'm finding it hard to work when he's there. It's distracting, always trying to overhear what he talks about, or where he is. I didn't want Pam to notice how I noticed him. I would die if she thought I liked him, she would tease me horribly and loudly!

Monday April 4

Guess Becky should have gone to see the principal on Friday. He was waiting for us when we got off the bus this morning, wearing his standard white short sleeved button down shirt—what a dork. Anyway, he didn't look at either of us, just spoke to the space between us.

"The school board decided it's in everyone's best interest if you…don't come back. I've been authorized to have the bus take you home." He coughed into his fist and put his hands in his pockets. "We wish you the best of luck."

I didn't know what to do. Becky stepped closer to me. I saw her smiling out of the corner of my eye. "Thank you, but I'll walk. Exercise is good for the baby."

I left with her, not giving him the chance to say anything else. We took our time, not talking for the first few blocks. For Becky to be that quiet I figured she was upset. When we got to the corner of White Street I let out a sigh.

"Don't worry about it Josie," she said and linked her arm through mine. "I'm okay. It's one less thing to stress about."

"Well, I'm pissed," I said.

"About me getting kicked out, or you having to go back alone?"

"You're so smart, no wonder you don't have to go back to school." Feeling better, I tugged her arm. "Fine, let's take the long way. You know, since exercise is *so* good for the baby."

We walked along the streets that ended or edged the Atlantic side of the island, starting with the White Street Pier until we hit the Southernmost Point and headed up Whitehead, to Fleming. The sun hasn't gotten super summer scorch-y, so we didn't have to keep crossing to be on the shady side of the street. Becky chatted about how Carol wanted to buy her a "real" sewing machine. But Becky said she wanted to try my grandmother's old one first. I didn't say much, just listened to her chatter.

I thought about school without her, and the reality sunk in—the news was out—Becky was pregnant. Becky was going to be a mother. Having so few memories of my own mother, I wasn't sure what to think about Becky being one. Funny, starting the year with thoughts of finding my own mother and here was Becky— mama to be—almost the same age as my mother when she was pregnant with me.

We stopped in Gil's to get stuff for dinner. Mike had to come to the register to do my employee discount. He wore blue and green plaid shorts and a light green Gil's Groceries polo. Between the shirt and his eyes, I thought he glowed. I could barely speak.

"Playing hooky?" He smiled. His eyes looked so bright when he smiled.

Not trusting my voice, I rolled my eyes.

Outside Becky elbowed me. "Cute."

I swallowed and faked a cough. "He's my boss."

"You're blushing," she sang.

"And ignoring you," I sang, and gave her the bag of groceries while I dug in my knapsack for my house key.

We made stir fried vegetables and fried tofu for dinner. I fried the tofu—I wouldn't let Becky get near the hot oil. Carol came over after work. Since Becky moved in she's been stopping by to see her. When Dad came in and saw the table all set and dinner cooking, he said, "Uh oh, who's in trouble? Me or one of you?"

"Funny," I said, and pulled out his chair.

He looked at Carol, "Now I'm really worried."

Over dinner Becky told them about the principal and us both leaving.

"Not surprising," Carol shook her head, her long silver earrings jingled lightly. "That place."

I hadn't even said anything, but Dad looked at me. "Don't even think about it Josephine. You're going back tomorrow."

"Seriously? Why? I could work more, help with expenses."

"No," both he and Carol said.

"You don't need to worry about that," Dad said.

"I know, I know," I exhaled. "You'll take care of me."

"Josie," Carol rubbed my shoulder. "Such a cliché, but you have plenty of time to work, and be an adult."

"Right, because being at school is such a laugh riot with all my friends and extracurricular activities."

"Seriously, Josie," Becky said. "It's only, like, two more months. Bring home assignments and stuff. I'll do the work with you. Then I can pretend I graduated too."

"You both will be graduates," Dad said. I didn't say anything. He got up to clear the table.

Wednesday April 6

Dad and TJ were at the kitchen table laughing when I came down this morning. TJ must have just gotten off shift—he had on his dark gray cargo pants, and gray *Paramedic* tee. *The Key West News* was on the table, TJ doodling on the headline.

Experts Discuss Ongoing O-meg Virus Outbreak

"That's right, let the Bubbas *discuss* things. That'll help," TJ said.

Dad laughed. "Probably down at 5 Brothers having a conference right now. I feel better already."

"How are you this morning, JJ?" TJ asked. He leaned back in his chair. The gray t-shirt stretched across his stomach. He's a big guy, not fat, but tall and wide. Height is another McKenzie trait.

"Oh great, I get to go to school again. What fun and intellectual stimulation will be in store for me today? Teachers ignoring me, kids crossing to the other side of the hall when they see me?"

Dad shook his head. TJ had his slanted smirky smile.

"Wait," I continued, waving my hands at them. "So, I gave up on the joys of gym. But the coach doesn't seem to have noticed. I haven't been called to the principal's office for skipping, so that's a plus." I gave them a thumbs up.

"That's the spirit, Josie," Dad said, standing up and lightly punching my shoulder. "Stay positive."

TJ finished his coffee and stood up. "It's so hard being young," he said. He gave me a side hug on his way to the sink.

I sighed. Adults can be so annoying.

The fun continues. From *The South Florida Times:*

President Diverts Ebola Funds to Fight O-meg

All day I wondered, what's worse—O-meg or Ebola? And I don't feel like asking Dad about that, might be TMI.

Monday April 11

A warm weekend—summer is coming. Judging by the quiet nights and empty parking spaces, the tourists and snowbirds have gone home. Season is over, if you could call it a season, as slow as it was this year.

At work Saturday afternoon Pam went home sick. When I went to the office to get a roll of quarters Mike was staring at the computer screen on his desk.

"I can work Pam's shift tomorrow if she doesn't feel better."

He looked up at me and the corners of his eyes relaxed.

"I wanted to give you time off on the weekends, for studying and hanging out."

"Give me a break," I told him. "I do all my studying at school since no one talks to me, and I don't '*hang out.*' I might as well work."

"You need time to be a teenager," he said. "You'll have plenty of time to work later on."

Great, another one, I thought.

"Like you?" He can't be that much older than me, and

yeah, probably not the best way to speak to my boss, but I'm tired of being treated like a kid. I don't think my life is very kid-like.

He shook his head and went back to the computer. "See you tomorrow then."

Turning away, I could hear a smile in his voice. I left the office quickly in case he looked back up and saw my own stupid grin.

Tuesday April 12

Becky had a doctor's appointment this morning. She told me about it on our walk to the White Street pier with the dogs. We sat on a bench facing the sunset. Pepper and Sargent raced down the pier and back to circle around us and go again. There weren't many people out.

"The doctor said everything looked...okay. He wonders if I'm wrong about the date of conception, because she's so small." Propping her sunglasses on top of her head, she turned to look at me. She was squinting, so I turned my body to face her instead of the setting sun.

"I am right about the date. That guy at Homecoming was the only other guy. Anyway, at my last appointment the doctor figured I was four months along. But this time he said she's the size of a four month old, but with the physical development of a seven month old."

I tried to follow, but I had no idea the difference between a four, or a five, or a seven month old baby.

"I didn't ask if that was good or bad. She's growing so it must be good, right?"

"Sure. So what does he know about pregnancies that might

be infected with O-meg?"

She rubbed her belly, a slight slope under her tank top. I put my hand on top of hers.

"Becky?"

She sighed. "I didn't tell the doctor anything about that. He never asked."

I kept my hand where it was. "Don't you think that's something he should know?"

"I did. Until I saw how everyone at school acted."

I squeezed her hand. "But, he's a doctor, you know, educated."

"Yeah, smart and educated like my mother? Or some of the creeps she works with?" She shook her head and stood up. "Unless it comes up, I'm not saying anything about the guy. Let the doctor think I'm just a teenage slut who has no idea who the father is."

"Come on," I said, standing up. Seeing us moving, the dogs came running.

"It's okay." She pulled her hair away from her face. "I know how I used to be, and how people saw me." She bent to scratch Sargent's back. "It's kind of funny, really. I was always so careful, and then this happens after sleeping with one guy, one time." She started to rub again. Reaching, I joined her. She smiled at me.

"Maybe she was meant to be."

With my hand on her cool soft belly I thought she might be right.

Wednesday April 13

Today at lunch I heard kids at the next table talking about

an O-meg debate they had in history class: Should the infected be quarantined?

Glad I skipped class. I saw Mr. Burke in the hall before lunch and he didn't say anything. I guess I can do what I want at this point, so I spend a lot of time in the library. The librarian is new this year, spends a lot of time in her office. I doubt she knows who I am, or anything about Becky. Becky was never much of a library-goer.

Friday April 15

Latest from *The South Florida Times:* **88 cases statewide.** I skimmed the article before putting the paper in the recycle bin, no mention of Monroe County. Maybe I'm starting to think like Dad but it seems AMG keeps giving numbers and printing scary headlines without actually providing information about any dangers or effects of O-meg.

Saturday April 16

Dad and TJ set up rain barrels in our backyard today. "It's not a well, but it'll do," Dad said.

"You know where to come if you ever need water," TJ assured him. Apparently my grandfather used to bottle water out of his well and sell it in the 1950s.

"It runs in my family to be prepared," Dad told me. Next, they're going to put solar panels on the roofs of both houses. I don't know if it's an environmental thing or a prepare- for-the-apocalypse thing.

Sargent's whimpering woke me up so I went to check on Becky. She was sitting up in bed crying.

"I dreamt about Dave," she told me. The room felt stuffy, so I turned on the AC window unit. The house was built way before air conditioning. My grandmother, Dad's mother, grew up in this house, and it was a big deal when they got electricity. They installed a huge ventilation fan in the attic that used to scare the crap out of me when I was little. It's like five feet tall. I wouldn't go up there, even when it was off. Now, I love it. By running the fan we don't have to use air conditioning as much and the house feels peaceful, all quiet, open and breezy.

Anyway back to Becky's dream. "He was in this big bubble, and it must've been really hot inside because he was just standing there, sweating. It poured down his face, soaking his shirt and shorts. He wasn't even trying to get out."

"It's hot where he is," I pushed the hair, damp at the temples, away from her face.

"Who knows where he is. I haven't heard from him in months. And even if he comes home now. What about her?" She patted her belly.

"Don't worry about that now. Just concentrate on you and your baby. The rest will work itself out."

"I still love him," she said quietly.

"I know. And you know he loves you."

"I hope so." She rubbed her belly. "You can turn off the AC, she seems to keep me cool."

The sun was just coming up, so I stayed with her until I heard Dad downstairs and smelled his blueberry banana pancakes.

Becky came down right after. Dad smiled, but didn't comment about how tired she looked.

"One cake, or two?" he asked.

Later, he went out to help someone trim their bougainvillea. He wore jeans, had on a long sleeved shirt and carried gloves. I reminded him to wear sneakers—I know from experience a bougainvillea thorn can easily pierce a flip flop. Becky and I worked in the garden out back under the shade sails Dad had put up, pulling weeds and snapping off dead leaves. It's been in the upper eighties all week in the afternoons. As we worked I asked Becky about Dave's family.

"They left soon after Dave went to basic training. His dad had retired from the Coast Guard, but he got called back and sent to the Panhandle." She got up and went to sit in the shade. "It's too early to be this hot," she said, placing her hands on her belly.

I kept pulling weeds, digging in to get the roots. The dirt felt cool and comforting. "Did you ever meet them?"

"Once, the night before Dave left. I wish I knew how to get in touch with them. I wonder if they've heard from him."

"You could try to find them."

"I don't know. Maybe no news is good news in this situation." She stood and started pulling dead leaves from one of the hanging spider plants.

"I think TJ works with a guy that was in the Coast Guard, maybe he could find out something about the stations in the Panhandle."

"Sure. I don't understand why his dad was called back. I thought retired meant retired." She shook her head. "Want some ice tea?" Not waiting for my reply she went in the house.

Sitting back on my heels, I wiped sweat off my forehead with the bottom of my t-shirt. It was too early to be this sweaty, drippy hot even in the shade.

Thursday April 21

Oh my god, will this week ever end? Or more accurately will this school year ever end??!!??! It's so boring without Becky. And a little weird that no one talks to me. Not that many ever did, but now it's deliberate. I've never been buddy buddy with anyone but Becky, but at least the teachers would acknowledge my existence, being one of the few who actually did homework and could answer questions. But not anymore.

So much for the summer-like sun. For the past four days it's only been in the mid-seventies, plus overcast. It's weird, cool and breezy with odd little showers throughout the day. People at work are hoping this will keep the ocean temperatures cool, meaning a quiet hurricane season.

Friday April 22

Full moon tonight. The bright light coming in through my window woke me up, and then a rooster crowed, as if greeting the day, reminding me that I love this island.

Sunday April 24

Becky and I spent the afternoon on the front porch brushing the dogs. It seems lately when I look out on the nearly empty streets of Old Town thoughts of my mother keep popping up making me wonder what it was about Key West that drove her away. I know she only transferred in during her junior year of high school when her father was hired as a chef at one of the fancy resort hotels. According to Carol my mother planned on going to college after graduation. Then, whoops, there I was!

Dad has always been insistent it was him she left, not me. But, what difference does it make? She's not here.

"How do you feel about staying here in Key West and raising a kid?" Running the brush over Pepper's head she closed her eyes. If she were a cat I think she would've purred.

"There's no place I'd rather be." She grabbed my hand. "I could not do this without you. I cannot do this without you." The weather had changed again with a heavy morning rain bringing on the humidity. My hand started to sweat.

I squeezed her hand that held the brush, but didn't look at her. "I'm not going anywhere." Sargent bumped her hand.

"I know, I know," she said and continued moving the brush down his back.

"I think you and the baby are good for my Dad."

"I think your father just loves to love, and now he feels like a big mama bear with a family of cubs to watch out for."

I laughed. "Are you going to call him 'mama bear' now?"

"God, no," she laughed. "But he has insisted I call him Robbie, no more Mr. McKenzie. It makes me feel kind of like an adult."

"Get used to it, Mama." A drop of sweat rolled down my neck.

"Here," she placed my hand on her shirt over her belly. It felt cool, and the feeling travelled up my arm and over my chest. It was wonderful and refreshing.

"That's awesome," I said, not adding my other thought—it was also a bit weird, but in a good way?

Monday April 25

The day started with Dad reading aloud from *The Key West News* after he finished his bucci shot:

Senator Smith Seeks Funding to Fight O-meg

"Considering she lives in South Florida it's about time," he said looking at me over the rim of his reading glasses.

"Do you think that'll help?" I got an ice cube from the freezer to cool my tea so I could drink it before leaving to catch the bus.

"I don't know, honey. I don't have much confidence they know what's going on."

"Do you? Know what's going on."

He put his little cup in the sink. He looked tired, still wearing the shirt from yesterday, a stretched out t-shirt with the profile of a green parrot head on the back.

"I think the paper's reporting on the spread of this supposed virus is inflated." He turned to face me. "And I'm no longer sure it's all about a virus. I've heard things about the babies being born to 'infected' mothers in some Latin American countries."

My stomach turned. "Like what?"

"It's not bad." He sat across from me at the table. "Apparently they're born early, around the seventh month. They're very small, but fully formed and healthy. One of my radio contacts, Raul, is in Colombia, and his wife's a nurse. She says the babies seem fine but the doctors say they're deformed or have birth defects. Then they keep them away from the parents, and even other nurses."

I wrapped my hands around my mug. He continued. "The wife is starting to help with home deliveries if there's a chance of it being an O-meg baby—that's what Raul calls them—O-megs."

"What about Becky?" I asked. "There's still the chance Becky is having…"

"Becky and her daughter will be fine." He looked down and seemed to notice his shirt.

"I'm going to change before doing the rounds."

"How often do these people come down to their 'properties' anymore?"

He laughed. "I didn't see any of them this season. But I saw their checks so I'll continue to treat their pools, wash their windows, and pressure wash their decks."

"What else did Raul say? What happens when the babies get older?"

He stood and kissed the top of my head. "We are all here. Becky and her daughter will be okay."

I believed him.

Good.

Even after time spent with Cloyal, and in the safety of their Municipality, it is difficult for Seeva to imagine a different beginning. One can imagine beginning in the hospitals of Colombia amongst flashing machines, stinging tests and glaring walls, separated. A cold environment, a lack of an environment, alone, Seeva knows.

First conscious in bright white and biting cold, surfaces hard and flat.

Many beings covered in loud yellow, many more eyes behind glaring glass.

Immobility, touches sensed but not felt, pierces and shocks felt.

Stomach turning unease, numbing fear.

A slowness, a ticking.

Covered faces dwindling, ticking never-ending.

How long until the last face came, but with no covering.

A snap of freedom, a crack in the white and the face disappearing into the darkness.

Seeva knew to wait, knew Cloyal was coming.

Friday April 29

A long, tiring week. I offered to work a couple of after-school shifts. Mike's also been working so that's nice. But it's been hot, like August hot, lower nineties during the afternoons. And today this was *The South Florida Times* headline:

Haiti Had O-meg Virus Months Before Brazil

Dad stopped by the store for brown rice at the end of my shift. I asked him about the headline while we walked home.

"I still think this is bigger than a virus. I just don't know how, like the news is trying to make it worse than it is."

A warm breeze blew down the street. Picking up a yellow frangipani blossom from the sidewalk, I tucked the flower behind his ear.

"First one of the season. It suits you," I said. He smiled and put his arm around me. I no longer wanted to think about viruses or Latin American countries, or Allied Media.

Sunday May 1

Becky declared this Hurricane Season Prep Month. By the time I got up she was in the kitchen—inventorying the cabinets. The counter and table top were full of cans and bags of beans, and she was making notes on a legal pad.

"Is this part of that nesting thing?" I asked her.

"Ha, ha." She didn't look up. "Hurricane season begins in a month. I want to be ready. My mother used to do this. I used to think she was being neurotic, but look at me now. I can't seem to stop." She did stop and look at me. "Maybe I'm more like her than I want."

I put the kettle on for tea. It felt like a strong black tea kind of morning. After grabbing a pack of peanut butter crackers out of the cupboard, I moved cans of chick peas and black beans aside and sat at the table.

"Right," I scoffed. "Get real, you are nothing like your mother."

Later, I sat on the floor poking around in the cabinet near the sink. It didn't look like anything Becky would need to list—old plastic grocery bags and zip lock bags.

"Have you been back to the doctor?" I couldn't see her face but her toes curled and flexed against the wood floor near where I sat.

"Nope, I feel all right." She ran water in the sink. "Your Dad gave me an old copy of *What to Expect When You're Expecting,* which hasn't been that helpful, I'll admit. Considering what the doctor said about her being small, and how I feel, I can't figure out much with the book. But I feel her. I know she's okay."

"Sure, and it's good for you to use that medical degree of yours." I shut the cupboard door and started to stand. Soapy water sprayed my back.

"Hey! It's raining Dawn scented drops in here!"

"Very funny. I don't want to go to a doctor unless something feels…off. Anyway, the doctor I went to hasn't called to check on me."

"Okay, but promise you'll let one of us know if anything starts to feel…I don't know…weird." She didn't turn from the sink.

"Sure," she said. "Okay." She still didn't turn around.

I started putting the cans of beans together in piles on the table.

Thursday May 5

Happy Cinco de Mayo!

And, Happy Birthday to me.

I turned eighteen today, now legally an adult, but I still have to finish high school.

For dinner we went to my favorite Mexican place on Stock Island. Sometimes it's hard to get Dad off Key West. If he has to go over Cow Key Channel, it's a big trip. Before I left to catch the bus this morning I reminded him to make sure he had his passport. He ha-ha'd me from behind the paper. No dramatic headlines today.

Dinner was awesome as usual. Dad and I always get the vegie fajita platter—it comes out on a sizzling cast iron pan, between that and the chips and salsa I usually leave feeling like I'm going to pop. The company was good, too—the whole family, or what feels like my family now.

Apparently, Carol had pestered Becky into going back to the doctor that afternoon. It didn't go well. He knew about the father being from somewhere in Latin America and possibly being O-meg positive.

"He was waiting on the porch outside his office when we walked up!" Carol squeezed the lime in her Dos Equis then tossed it into the glass. A little beer splashed out and she licked the lime off her fingers. "He went off about patient-doctor privilege, or something, and how Becky had jeopardized the cleanliness and reputation of his practice." Carol's face was pink, clashing with her red hair. "What an ass…jerk."

She smiled at Becky. "I'm trying to watch my language so the baby won't think I'm a foul mouth. Or worse, learn to talk like me."

Becky didn't seem upset about the doctor, or Carol's language. But she was folding a torn piece of napkin in half again and again like she'd done with the toilet paper that day in the school bathroom.

"Aunt Carol, you're fine. She'll learn to swear from someone and I'd rather it be you."

Carol hooted with laughter.

Becky declared, "For now, no more doctors."

I took the tiny wad of paper from her and handed her the basket of chips.

"Okay, Mama," I said. "Anyone want more chips?"

Later, I was in bed reading my gift from Dad, *The Scarlet Letter*, inscribed:

Don't read too much into this, it was next on the shelf.

Birthdays in my family are celebrated with a meal and something silly or re-gifted. Since I turned 13 Dad and TJ have taken a book off one of their own shelves, re-inscribed it to me and wrapped it up.

Becky came in with a box wrapped in newspaper. "Look," she said. "I wrapped and recycled at the same time."

Not wanting her to see it, I slid the novel under the sheet by my thigh. Her gift was a box of blank moleskin journals, each with a different color cover. She sat on the bed and pulled them out of the box.

"I got them at that new/used bookstore up the street. The plain black covers looked so boring. The owner special ordered these."

I ran my hands over the grainy covers. I love my plain black and white composition notebook but these felt...serious. I would wait to use these.

"It's been cool to see you writing so much. I thought you could write about us, maybe you already are. I want you to keep writing about everything, about me and my baby, no matter what. I want someone to read about us someday and know, I don't know...."

Grabbing her in a hug, I saw my composition book on the bedside table, a pen sticking out, not even a quarter full.

"I will."

I have to, I thought. I don't know if I will ever have the courage to leave, especially now, but someone has to know about us down here.

Friday May 6

Dad was waiting for me when I dragged myself into the house after school today. School, it's been…forget it…this is much more interesting.

So Dad sat at the big table rubbing his thumb lightly over the swirls and curves of the wood grain. He looked serious. He stared at the table and didn't look up at me when I sat across from him with a glass of water.

"Everything okay?" I asked, I didn't see any newspapers laying around so I figured there wasn't a national crisis, or scandal.

"I hope you won't be mad at me." He pulled an unopened letter from the breast pocket of his faded flowered shirt, a Key West camouflage print, as he called it.

"This came the day before your birthday and I held it. I'm sorry, I didn't want you to have to deal with…whatever this is on your birthday. And I wanted to give it to you, I didn't want you to just find it in the mailbox."

The letter from my mother was on the table, a regular business sized envelope with a return address somewhere in Georgia, handwritten.

"Is this her handwriting?" I asked. "I don't even know what her handwriting looks like."

"It's her."

So confused, I couldn't remember that this was something

I wanted, to find my mother after more than ten years. I wasn't expecting her to want to find me.

Pushing the letter closer to me across the table, Dad said, "It's your letter, JJ. Open it when you feel ready."

I wondered if I should be alone? Should I be with Becky? Should I stay with Dad? I stood and went out to sit on the front steps, close to everyone. I put the envelope up to my nose, but it smelled like Dad, the aloe soap he used, I guess from being in his shirt pocket. That made me feel good. Carefully tearing along the top seam, I slid out the piece of paper, more unfamiliar hand writing on Southern Gas letterhead.

> Dear Josie,
>
> First, Happy Birthday. I figured it was time. I know nothing about you, but I do know you are now 18.
> I don't know if you'll understand, especially after so much time, but I had to get away. Not from you, but from there, from that time. My life was not going as expected, and I needed a break. I loved you so much, but didn't know what to do. I did know your father loved you, he was so devoted. I never doubted he would be the better parent. I'm sorry to bring this up now but I think you're old enough, I think I'm old enough. I know you can take care of yourself. And your father, take care of him too. I'm glad you've had each other these years.
> Love,
>
> Mom

So there it was. While I thought about finding my mother, she found me. Although, she knew where to look, knew from the day she left where to find me.

According to *The South Florida Times* there are three new cases. Again, no mention of where. I think Miami-Dade County? Ugh, part of me doesn't even care at this point. Seriously, until Becky gives birth I don't want to get all wound up.

And speaking of getting wound up, Mike wished me a belated happy birthday at work today. I went to the office for my cash drawer at the beginning of my shift and he smiled when he saw me, like showed teeth and everything, then told me I would be on register two and added, "Hope you had a nice birthday."

And what did I say?

Nothing.

I just took the cash drawer out of his hands and headed to register two.

Yeah, real mature. I'm an adult now. (Just like it's real mature of me to ignore the letter from my mother.)

Sunday May 8

I guess the whole family has started to nest? Becky had a list and we spent the entire day in hurricane prep mode. Dad and TJ worked on TJ's house and their boat—getting new lines and stuff like that. They didn't go out much, but when their schedules and the weather cooperate, we eat fresh fish for days.

Carol, Becky and I trimmed and swept around our house, then headed out to New Town for stock-up shopping. That's when I decided to tell them about the letter. Yes, after going up and down aisles at Publix loading our cart with peanut butter, cans of tuna, and granola bars I said, "I got a letter from my mother the day after my birthday." (Leaving out the part about Dad holding onto it for a couple of days.)

We were in the bottled water aisle, Carol having just returned with another cart, Becky leaning down to grab a 2 ½ gallon container of water. As if in slow motion, they both stopped and turned very slowly to face me. Taking the container of water from Becky, I said, "Yeah, happy birthday to me." Becky stared at me, but Carol smiled.

"It was on Southern Gas letterhead. Are you still in touch with her?"

"Yes," she said. "We've been friends since high school."

"I knew that, I just never thought…has she asked about me over the years?"

"Only asked that I tell her if there were ever any problems. I didn't know she was going to write to you."

"So you never told her there was a problem with a woman leaving her six year old daughter?" Becky asked, kind of loudly.

"It's okay, Becky, Carol isn't the one who left."

Becky put her hand over her stomach, which still hardly looked like anything more than that—just a slightly rounded belly. Feeling exhausted, I almost wished I hadn't brought it up. The store was getting busy, and we now had a cart full of hurricane supplies along with Carol's additional cart full of bottled water.

Becky turned to me, "Josie, talk to me about this, whenever, wherever."

Trying to lighten the mood, I motioned to the bright aisle filling with others loading up with bottled water.

"Done," I said.

So I no longer feel like I have to find her. I feel…peaceful?

I don't know, but I do feel better about something, like maybe now I can just stay here, stay on the island with Dad, and Becky, and the baby.

Monday May 9

I worked this afternoon then Becky pestered me with questions about Mike, maybe trying to distract me from mother thoughts? Anyway, I didn't give her much.

"What was he wearing?"

"A Gil's Groceries shirt like everyone else." *It was dark green making his eyes look brighter than normal.*

"Did he talk to you?"

"Yes, Becky, or course he talked to me, he's my boss." *Every time he went by my register he asked if I needed anything, coins, small bills, bags.*

"You like him, don't you?"

"He's okay." *I like him. I really like him.*

Tuesday May 10

Today's headline from *The South Florida Times* caused all kinds of chit chat at Gil's:

Keys Residents Oppose Fighting O-meg With Genetically Altered Mosquitos

Mike was working a register when I got there. I had my cash drawer and waited to take his place. The customer, a woman buying three bags of key limes, said something about Big Brother science messing with Mother Nature.

"Over mosquitos!" She shook her head putting her change in the pocket of her long sun dress. "Today's youth, thinking they're so smart, messing with Mother Nature." She looked at me where I stood behind Mike.

"Don't blame her," Mike said with a laugh, nudging me with his elbow. "This is Robert McKenzie's daughter!"

She smiled and nodded. "Okay. Robbie, he's okay," she said. "He always sweeps off my roof before the summer rains begin. He knows what's what" She grabbed her limes and left.

"Been like that all day?" I asked. He took his cash drawer out and made room for me.

"Off and on," he said and touched the small of my back as I moved in behind the register. I held my breath. "You can handle it."

I exhaled as he walked away.

I felt that spot on my back for hours.

Friday May 13

A storm started brewing in the Gulf, just above the Yucatan headed for the Keys, and this year's Hurricane Preparedness guide showed up at the store today, timely—if people can cram it all into a couple of days. Gulf storms usually don't pop up until September, and they can be *fast*. Already this one is predicted to hit us on Monday, hopefully as not much more than a strong tropical storm. I'm not going to let the fact that I heard about this on Friday the 13th freak me out. But, I am planning to pay a visit to the Grotto at St. Mary's Basilica with Dad and Becky tonight, maybe light a few extra candles?!

Yesterday's hurricane tip was to *Determine Your Risk*. Done—we're at risk. Bonnie became a tropical storm yesterday, today a hurricane, briefly.

Today's tip: *Develop an Evacuation Plan*. Well, that wasn't necessary—there was no time to leave, plus Dad has never evacuated, his family never evacuated. We have no "Evacuation Plan." Our plan is to stay, no matter what.

So we spent the day in the living room. School was cancelled, once the winds are forecast to go above 35 mph they can't have the buses going over the bridges. Carol stayed with us, TJ was working at the hospital. Early in the day, after a big clap of thunder, flash of lightening and whoosh of wind the lights cut out and the ceiling fans slowed, then stopped. Silence lay under the wind as all air conditioning units in the neighborhood stopped. Dad looked over at me and through the sliver of light still coming in from the back windows I thought he winked.

"This is just a tropical storm. The power can go out during a strong cold front in the winter or a hot day during season when all the snowbirds run their ACs. Who wants to play cards?"

The odd mechanical voice of the weather radio blended with the wind, rustling trees and broken branches hitting the roof. There were no crashes, cracks of wood, or shattering glass. We got used to the noise. Pepper and Sargent did not. They spent the day under one of the upholstered chairs in the living room.

As we played cards around the kitchen table, I tried to not think of Mike. He lives like a block away with his Uncle Gil. Knowing he heard the same thing as me—the same wind and rain and similar tree branches coming down—I wondered what he did once the power went out.

According to the weather radio, at one point the wind did hit 78 mph with gusts up to 90. So, yes, we had a hurricane, a Category 1, before hurricane season even officially started, already knocking off two names—Alex and Bonnie. Great.

Wednesday May 18

I guess Bonnie wasn't that bad, a bunch of branches and palms came down but no actual trees. I spent Tuesday sweeping and raking the sidewalk and front yard, hoping to see Mike. The power was back on that afternoon. A sailboat pulled anchor and ran into the tie line. The Internet was still out, even during the scheduled hours at school, no connection. Yes, I was back at school. Maybe we lit too many candles at the Grotto. Mary kept us way too safe. I could've used another day off.

The latest thing has been for no one to talk around me. As in no one even talks to each other when I'm around. Complete silence. It makes for a very quiet bus ride.

You're welcome, I want to tell the bus driver when we get to school. Only a week and a half left of this.

Thursday May 19

I needed a treat before getting on the bus this morning so I went to the Cuban coffee place for a Chai tea. While waiting in line Dad came up behind me and put *The Key West News* in front of my face.

I jumped. "Geez Dad, can't I get some tea first?"

"Oh come on, it's kind of funny," he said. I looked at the

headline:

CDC Director – O-meg Bill Inadequate

"It's so cute when they try to get serious," he said.

"Be nice."

"We know what's really going on anyway."

"We do?" I asked.

"Well, okay not really, but we know more is going on than they're reporting. We know not to believe them and that's more than others know…you know?"

I laughed. "Have an extra bucci this morning, Dad?"

"Ha-ha," he said and pointed to the back page of the paper with more about Hurricane Preparedness Week. "Since we're making jokes. Look, tomorrow we need to *Identify Trusted Sources of Information for a Hurricane Event.*"

He left with a backwards wave. "That'll be easy, there are none!"

The thin woman at the counter gave me an extra shot of cinnamon. "Your Dad's funny," she said. She had four nose rings in her right nostril. "You're lucky."

I put an extra dollar in the tip jar.

"I know."

Sipping my spicy warm tea on the very quiet bus, I repeated her words over and over, *you're lucky. I'm lucky.* Since my mother's letter, I realize she didn't just leave me when I was six years old. She left me with Dad. She knew he would take care of me, probably better than she could have. Maybe her leaving was a sign of love.

Becky and I spent the day cleaning up the backyard and garden. It got a bit torn up from Bonnie. Mike was working so I knew there was no chance of him walking by. If we'd been out front I'm sure Becky would've noticed if I kept looking in the direction of his street.

TJ stopped by looking for Dad. When he saw us in the garden he reminded us that his grandfather used to say even if we lost the bridges we could still survive off the island and surrounding ocean.

"Don't forget all the added meat sources on dry land—iguanas, chickens, raccoons, possums and rabbits," he said.

"Great," Becky and I said at the same time. Becky pulled a long vine off the basil and rosemary.

TJ laughed. "Hey, don't forget the goats over on the navy base."

"Thanks, TJ," I said with a wave. "I'll tell Dad you stopped by."

"Just trying to make you feel better," he said.

"Sure, Tio," I said with another wave.

Thankfully he left. His laugh followed him out of the yard.

"TMI," Becky said. "Way TMI."

"You think?" I said, repeating again, *I am lucky.*

Tuesday May 24

Noticed something weird at school today. Sasha and her crew weren't around. I don't think I've seen them since before the tropical storm. They were never the most scholarly bunch but why quit this close to the end?

Friday May 27

It is over. Maybe not officially. There're some half days next week, but no matter what I do at this point—I will not fail out of high school. A diploma will be mailed to me sometime in June.

No one in the administrative offices were surprised or upset that I had no plans on participating in any graduation events or "celebrations." The principal's office door was closed, no big farewell for me.

Good riddance Key West High and class of 2016.

Sunday May 29

Another storm, out in the Atlantic, really strong—a Category 3—but not around any land. Hurricane Colin. Three down.

Tuesday May 31

Nothing from Colin, it swirled around the shipping lanes before heading north.

Then, right on time, an article in the paper about this year's hurricane season—more named storms than average, more "major" storms than past years. Blah, blah, blah. At least it's a change from headlines and articles about viruses and mosquitos. At Gil's everyone was talking hurricanes and tropical storms, evacuations and generators. Mike asked me if I would ever leave. I just looked at him.

He smiled. "Right, the McKenzies don't leave," he said. I

loved his smile, forcing his eyes to squint at the outer corners.

Anyway, here are the names for this hurricane season:

- Alex (Remember Alex, from like SIX months ago!?)
- Bonnie (Yeah, we remember Bonnie, she was like JUST here.)
- Colin (check)
- Danielle
- Earl
- Fiona
- Gaston
- Hermine
- Ian
- Julia
- Karl
- Lisa
- Matthew
- Nicole
- Otto
- Paula
- Richard
- Shary
- Tobias
- Virginie
- Walter

―――――

The page is marked with a tab of colored paper, the top creased and tattered. Seeva notes most of the names are crossed out.

There is thunder in the distance, faint.

First official day of hurricane season and Mother Nature has wasted no time. Hello Tropical Storm Danielle, way out in the Atlantic. The five day forecast only takes her through the Lesser Antilles. We have to wait and see. Let the hurricane tracking begin!

Thursday June 2

Bad headline from *The Key West News* today:

Baby Born in US with O-meg has Defect

Becky takes Pepper and Sargent for a walk every morning. There's a newspaper box on the corner. This headline was above the fold. She must have seen it.

Thinking of her distracted me at work. I had to call for a void like 3 or 4 times, entering the wrong code for bananas, double scanning something. For the first time I didn't want to be there. I checked on her as soon as I got home. Pepper met me at the door. I figured Sargent was with Becky. Her bedroom door was closed.

She didn't open when I knocked, just called out "I'm fine, just tired." Her voice sounded muffled and far away.

Dad told me about the article at dinner. I'd made chick pea salad with tomatoes and cucumbers—way too much, Becky loves chick peas, but she didn't join us.

"Typical story with lots of speculation and no facts," he said. "Nothing about where the baby was born, or anything about the parents. Not even any mention of what type of defect."

Pepper lay on the floor under the table, I rubbed her side with my bare foot.

"I got in touch with Raul on the radio this afternoon," he told me. "His wife was fired from the hospital but still helps women with home births. She hasn't seen any types of defects, but they're not really normal either." He put his hand under the table and snapped. Pepper got up and went to him. She left a warm spot on the wood floor where I rested my foot. He continued. "They are born early and so small they look like a tiny child or doll. And all she's seen so far are girls. Raul thinks the Latin American Front has more to do with containment than protecting US oil interests."

As I picked up the plates I asked, "But what is there to contain?"

"I don't know," he pushed away from the table. "I think the government is just scared of anything they don't understand."

Since I cooked he started to wash the dishes, I went upstairs to check on Becky again. "Night" was all she said in reply to my knock. Later, I woke up to a warm spot at the foot of my bed where Pepper sleeps and heard Becky leaving with the dogs. Midnight dog walk on a Thursday, good time to be alone.

Friday June 3

I didn't see Becky at all today. I had to work, and it was busy with people stocking up, or restocking, for our new hurricane—Danielle. Bottled water, canned stuff, peanut butter, and beer, beer, beer. Everyone was busy, I only saw Mike as he rushed by to put out more bottled water or box up someone's big order for one of the cashiers. The day flew by, he was still in the office with Gil when Pam and I left. She lit a cigarette as soon as the door slid shut and locked behind us.

"Damn, I'm tired. I sure hope all this is just an overreaction," she blew the smoke away from me and turned towards the parking lot. I wanted to look back in the store and see if Mike was coming out.

"Have a good night," she said.

"You too."

When I got home I noticed Dad had put a hurricane tracking map on the fridge, a pencil spot on the latest coordinates for Danielle. She'd sped up with the center just past the Lesser Antilles. The weather radio's creepy mechanical voice added to the quiet anticipation in the house. At least the shutters were still open. Dad waits until the last possible moment before closing them.

Staring intently at the map, I jumped when someone spoke.

"Hey, Josie." Carol laughed. "Shit, sorry. I thought you saw me when you came in. How can you miss this hair?" She motioned with a knitting needle to the magenta red shade of her spikey cut. "I had it touched up today, part of my hurricane preparations."

She sat on the couch, knitting. After pouring two glasses of iced tea, I sat next to her.

"Your Dad is out helping one of the neighbors with plywood. Buying, cutting, putting up? I can't remember." She didn't look at me, instead concentrated on the slow uneven movement of the knitting needles.

"How's she doing?" I asked, pointing to the ceiling.

"When I knocked she said she was resting. She'd taken the dogs for a long walk this morning. Sargent's still with her. He doesn't like to be away from her."

"Yeah, that's been going on for a while." Through the open back door I saw Pepper laying in the shade of a mini-mango tree

Dad planted last month.

"I used to knit in college," Carol said. "A nice break from studying. It's coming back to me." She held up a small piece made of purple yarn, not quite a square, but not round enough to be a circle. She looked at me. "Okay, maybe it's coming back slowly."

"You think?" I laughed. "At least it's not pink."

"Oh, I remembered your aversion as a child. Your mother told me she had to return a pair of pink sneakers she bought when you were learning to walk. You'd sit down and refuse to walk whenever she put them on you. She finally exchanged them for a light blue pair with a cloud design."

I thought I might tense up the first time Carol mentioned my mother, but I just drank my tea. I remembered the first pair of sneakers Dad bought me after she left—neon green Converse.

"Anyway, I'm going to knit all kinds of baby things over the next two months."

In the stillness of the house, as the weather radio droned more coordinates and wind speeds, I couldn't help but wonder if it would really be another two months.

Saturday June 4

Becky went into labor tonight. It was after dinner. Dad and I were cleaning up when Sargent started barking. We rushed upstairs. Becky's bedroom door was open, and the bathroom door closed. Sargent barked and scratched at the door jam. Dad didn't knock. Becky sat in the bathtub crying. Sargent pushed by him and licked her sweaty face.

"I don't feel good," she said, her voice shaky. "It can't be time yet, right? It's too early. It can't be time."

"I don't know, darling." He held her wrist for a few seconds, her arms shiny with sweat. Finally he looked at me and mouthed the words *too fast*. I ran downstairs and dialed TJ's pager, then called Carol.

"I just called TJ," I told her. "I don't know if it's time or what. She's really sweaty and her pulse is racing."

"Well, crap," she exclaimed. "No baby clothes from Auntie. I'll be right over."

Halfway up the stairs I stopped, hearing Becky cry. "She's not defective. She's just a baby."

Sargent whined. I heard Dad's voice, but couldn't make out what he said. The phone rang, so I turned and jumped back down the last two steps.

It was TJ. "On my way," he said. I heard static and street noises before he hung up.

"He's coming," I called out as I ran back upstairs and went into Becky's room. Newspapers from the last three days were on her bed and all over the floor. I grabbed her favorite hoody, dark brown with ARMY across the front, and a pair of thick red socks. I had no idea what she would need. Downstairs, the front door slammed open. I met TJ half way up the stairs.

"Hallway bathroom," I said.

I made it to the top of the stairs before TJ came out of the bathroom carrying Becky wrapped in a large beach towel. Dad was holding Sergeant back. I gave him the sweatshirt and socks, and took hold of Sargent's collar.

"You stay here," he told me. "We're taking her to the hospital and I don't want a crowd drawing attention."

I nodded.

"Is Carol coming over?" He was almost at the bottom of the stairs. My fingers hurt from griping Sargent's collar as he pulled and whimpered.

"Carol is coming," I said as the door slammed behind him. Sargent pulled out of my grip and ran down the stairs. He barked and scratched at the door. I sat on the top step holding my knees. Once Sargent had quieted down to a low growl with his nose pressed to the base of the door, Pepper came out of my room and nudged her wet nose under my arm. She rested her head against my thigh and let out a warm sigh of dog breath against my skin. I put my face into her fur. She needed a bath. Maybe I would give her one tonight, I thought. That's what I wanted to think about at that moment. The dogs needed a bath.

Sunday June 5

Becky and the baby came home this morning. She was born late last night, soon after they got to the hospital. I hadn't slept all night, especially after giving Pepper and then Sargent a bath. It was a great distraction filling the tub, wrestling the dog into the tub, cleaning the bathroom of sprayed water and soap suds. Repeat. By the time I finished wiping everything down for the second time, I noticed the sky getting lighter and heard Dad downstairs filling the espresso pot with water. I ran out to the top of the stairs and stopped when I saw Becky's head over the back of the couch. Hearing Dad at the stove I inhaled and felt a bit dizzy knowing they were both home, doing what they do on a normal day—sitting on the couch, making coffee. Only a few lights were on, Carol slept in the recliner in the dark corner by the back door.

Dad started talking as I descended the stairs, and then I could see Becky held a large bundle of pink blanket.

"It was quick," he said, just above a whisper. "The place was crowded and crazy with staff and National Guard getting critical patients evacuated before Danielle. TJ, in his uniform, carrying Becky, slid into a cubicle in the emergency room, unnoticed. I followed like I belonged there and pulled the curtain behind me." He got one of his small white cups from the cupboard.

"Next thing we knew, there she was—so tiny. She felt cool when I picked her up but her eyes were open, looking at me," he continued. Steam pushed out of the pot on the stove, he turned off the burner. "We took a cab home. TJ is still at the hospital, helping out."

I went to Becky. She didn't seem to be listening.

"There was no pain," she said to me. "It was so fast, and she's so tiny, like a little doll."

Sitting next to them, I pulled back the blanket to see a light brown face, like the size of a small grapefruit, a sheen of hair lighter than her skin, and eyes almost black. I felt airy with relief, like my arms could float. I touched her cool check. Her lips tipped up at the corners.

Tucking the blanket around her head I commented, "Pink, Becky, really?"

"God, J, it's from the emergency room. All the blankets are pink." She spoke just above a whisper. Laying my head on her shoulder, I heard the smile in her voice.

"All right," I said quietly. "She can have pink, this once."

Her eyes were still open watching me.

"All those crazy headlines. All that drama, over such a tiny being."

She named her Evelyn, after my Dad's mother.

———

How would that have felt?

Warm, comforted, safe from the beginning. Seeva goes out to look at the abandoned, flooded waterways where streets used to be, where humans used to live. Thunder continues. The gray horizon darkens while the sea churns with white caps.

Seeva still feels Cloyal's presence, searching, but not close. Seeva leaves the view and returns to read.

Monday June 6

Not to be forgotten—Danielle picked up speed, rolling up towards Puerto Rico, Haiti, Dominican Republic and forecast to just skim Cuba, no weakening expected, already a strong Category 1, moving fast over warm water, should be here in about three days.

Welcome to Key West, Evie!

Tuesday June 7

Work was crazy. Even Mike and Gil were on the floor all day restocking and helping. Dad spent yesterday making sure all the properties he manages were secure, then today he and Carol worked on the outside of our house, securing lawn furniture, making sure the shutters would shut and latch. They did the same at TJ's. The boat was still tied up and secure from the last storm so

TJ just double checked it before heading to the hospital. Becky put Evie in a baby sling around her chest and went to work in the house getting candles, checking batteries and flashlights, freezing bottles of water, and cleaning out coolers.

She told me later she thought Evie would sleep, but every time she looked down she was wide eyed and watching.

Wednesday June 8

Gil's only stayed open til six. The weather is supposed to start deteriorating around midnight. Latest forecast has Danielle as a Category 2 hurricane with the eye going over the lower Keys tomorrow.

At closing, Gil stayed behind to take care of some last minute preparations. Mike and I left at the same time. After locking the door Mike caught up and walked down the street with me.

"It's supposed to start getting bad after midnight," he said.

"I'm going to the Grotto at St. Mary's after dinner, just to be safe."

"Yeah? Gil used to do that." There was no one else around, walking or driving, so we could've walked down the middle of the street.

"I guess a lot of people evacuated? It's so quiet. I love it." I could hear the high pitch of a scooter wailing down the next block.

"Won't be quiet for long if it's anything like the last one," he said.

"This one is stronger. Do you wish you left?" I asked. The green of our *Gil's Groceries* shirts looked really good on him with his almost blonde hair and Florida boy tan.

"Not really. If Gil thinks it's safe, I feel okay. He's been here about as long as your family. When I was younger my mom would leave if a hurricane was coming. We'd just go back to Naples early. But, we were here for a few tropical storms." We'd reached his corner. He kept talking. "What about your Dad? I've heard he's very resourceful. You'll be fine."

"I know," I said.

"Well, good luck," he said. I just stood there. Before she left Pam had hugged both Mike and Gil when she wished them luck. But Pam was practically family—used to watch Mike when Gil first brought him to the store as a little kid. My hug would have been different from hers. I don't know if Mike would know that.

"You too," was all I said and jogged across the street towards my house.

Later, on the way to the Grotto, Becky let me carry Evie in the shoulder sling. She was so light, like carrying nothing. TJ wasn't on duty yet, and Carol had been hanging with us a lot since Evie arrived.

All the candles in glass were lit, and others were stuck into the rocks or on the ground. Carol lit a tea light candle. I left a frangipani blossom. Becky watched Evie, blinking as she looked at all the candles.

"Hey, Mary," Dad said, placing his hand on one of the coral rocks that made up the structure. "We're back."

Meanwhile, the virus was still out there, making news. Saw this headline on *The South Florida Times* on our way back:

Miami is 'Ground Zero' For Outbreak of O-meg Virus, Doctor Warns

Dad put his arm around my shoulders. "Starting to wonder what all the fuss is about," he said.

A small gust of wind hit us as we rounded the corner of Fleming and I wondered what Mike was doing at that very moment.

Thursday June 9

Hurricane Danielle spent the day with us, like the whole day, and into the night. The power went out early afternoon. We were all in the living room. It felt safer to stay together like last time. It can be unnerving, the varying volume of wind, while feeling like you're waiting for that one big crash, that one big shatter of a tree or roof coming down with every gust.

I sat on the end of the couch, a book in my lap, not sure what to do once the power went out, not feeling like getting up to change positions or get a flashlight. Carol was on the floor by a window trying to knit by the light filtered through the shutter.

Dad turned his chair to face the uncovered window onto the back yard and tried to read a paper. Becky and Evie lay on the couch. They couldn't have been sleeping with all the noise of wind and falling branches. Plus, I noticed Evie's eyes were open, looking at me. The room was stuffy. I put my hand on her head but she felt cool. She smiled and I felt a chill go through me from the top of my own head. I breathed out, relaxed and smiled back at her.

"Been a long time since we've had a storm like this," Dad said as the wind picked up to a steady low whistle. He raised his voice over the storm noise. "Maybe since the season before you were born."

"Like maybe nine months before she was born?" Becky asked, her eyes still shut. I knew she wasn't asleep. There was a loud whoosh of wind, and it felt like the house inhaled. Evie closed her eyes briefly. I removed my hand from her head and turned the book over in my lap.

"Gross. Stop it," I said holding the book up to my face.

"Your mother claimed you were born a month early." Dad was looking out the window. I could see the light weight bamboo where the tomatoes were staked, rippling in the wind gusts.

"Ugh," I said, and moved to the cushioned swivel chair, turning it to face the wall. The last thing I wanted during a major hurricane was to hear funny stories about my mother. At least TJ was at the hospital so he couldn't join in the reminiscing. Closing my eyes, I wondered if this was what cabin fever felt like. A crack of thunder and a flash of light ended the joke fest.

When Dad finished reading the paper he got out a Coleman lamp and we all played Uno. We didn't keep score, just played game after game until Becky noticed the silence.

"Listen," she said.

Dad stood up. "The eye."

"I want to go out," I said. Becky went to the front door and opened it a crack, she cradled Evie in her other arm. Turning to me, she smiled and opened the door wide. The sky glowed yellow through light cloud cover, like it was really glowing. Palm fronds and trees branches hardly moved in the breeze and it was quiet—no planes, no cars or mopeds, no air conditioners, no wind.

At that moment Dad turned up the weather radio as the robotic voice announced the eye was over Key West.

"Come on," he said. "We'll only go a couple of blocks. We

stay together. And wear sneakers, no flip flops—who knows what's fallen into the street."

Carol slapped her cards face down on the table. "But I was winning!" She tugged up her yoga pants and grabbed the dogs' leashes. No one put on raincoats except Becky. She tucked Evie into her sling and zipped the coat up to her little face so she could see. We left the door open behind us. Outside the air was still and heavy but not as thick as inside the house.

Once outside, the dogs peed for about 30 seconds before we headed in the direction of White Street. Sargent walked in front of Becky and Evie. Pepper stayed next to me. Plywood or shutters covered the windows of most of the houses we passed. Also metal hurricane shutters, and on a few of the fancy remodeled houses— the heavy plastic kind you could see through. No one really lived in any of those houses, I don't know why they bothered.

Green leaves covered everything like a carpet. Branches of all sizes were down. A huge mahogany tree had fallen and blocked the street three blocks from the house. Power lines tangled in the top most branches and dipped close to the pavement. That's where we turned around and headed back.

It felt other worldly-the yellow glow, the calm, the silence. We didn't even talk amongst ourselves. At the house, I kept walking towards Gil's house. Becky followed, Dad and Carol stood back kicking downed branches and palm fronds out of the street. I stopped at the corner. Gil and Mike were looking at a large tree that had fallen on the porch roof of a house across the street. Mike turned in my direction. It looked like his face relaxed, and he smiled, putting his hand on his chest. I swear it was over his heart. I smiled at him, thankful for the silence. Then the wind picked up from the opposite direction. The eyewall would hit soon. Becky and I headed home, still not speaking.

Friday June 10

Still wet and windy today, but it started to calm down in the late morning. Thank you Danielle for over 24 hours of wind of differing strengths—howling, whistling and shrieking. Dad turned up the weather radio. The worst had passed, and she was heading into the Gulf. I imagine no power for a while, but the phone land line works. We all gave up on cell phones a while ago. TJ came home from the hospital. They closed up once the power went out. He checked in with us before heading to his house.

"All good, brother," Dad told him on the porch. When I went out to see him, super dark circles were under his eyes. He held me in a big hug, warm, but I didn't pull away.

"See you for dinner. And, congratulations, graduate."

Oh yeah, tonight would have been graduation, except we got hit by a hurricane instead. So no one walked tonight. Hmm, graduation ceremony or hurricane, which would have been worse?

Later, we had a dinner of peanut butter on crackers, cold peas from a can and V8. No one had the energy to get too creative yet.

"We'll have to break out that *Apocalypse Chow* cook book," Carol said. "See what kind of gourmet meals we can cook with no electricity." Becky held a pea up to Evie—no response. She then tossed the pea at my Dad where he sat on the couch. After it bounced off the top of his head he sat up and turned around.

"Ahem," Becky fake coughed.

"Oh, right!" He jumped up and rummaged in the closet by the back door, then handed me a roll of newspaper, twisted at both ends. "Pardon the wrapping, it's been a little hectic the last few days."

It was a red and white graduation tassel.

"It was your mother's. She must've left it behind. I found it in that box of books from the closet in Becky's room."

"Thank you." I didn't know where to look, so I stared at my hands and combed my fingers through the red and white strands across my palm. *She left a lot behind,* I thought, *a long time ago.* Behind the storm clouds the sun was setting, and the room was getting dark. TJ lit the tall taper candles in the middle of the table.

"We wanted to have a little ceremony for you both," he said.

Becky and I shook our heads.

"We're good," she said. "Done and don't have to go back."

I lay the tassel in my lap and we clinked our tiny cans of V8. "Exactly."

"Game of gin everyone?" Dad shuffled a deck of cards.

This is good. Everything I need is here, I thought, inhaling the faint scent of Sandalwood from the tassel in my lap. The image of Mike standing in the middle of the street with his hand to his heart came to me and my breath caught.

Saturday June 11

Still squally but the wind died down last night. As soon as it started to get light, Dad opened the house up—opened the shutters, opened the windows, opened the doors. The wind was still warm and damp but it moved through the house. They used to pay more attention to building in order to keep houses cool, naturally.

Carol left to go home but was back soon.

"Sauna," she exclaimed. She lives in a condo down the street, first floor middle of the row. "Move over, Mama." She lay on a sheet covered braided rug on the other side of Becky. Evie was on her chest. Dad slept on the couch.

I curled up facing Becky and looked at Evie. There were trees to cut up, leaves to sweep, houses to check but now we needed to rest, to sleep for hours uninterrupted by claps of thunder, flashes of lightening, gusts of wind, crashes of branches. The last thing I remembered seeing was Evie's tiny hand tucked under her tiny head, her eyes open, everyone sleeping but her.

Monday June 13

Yesterday was a solid day of clean up—sweeping, raking, bagging leaves and small branches, dragging larger branches to the curb. Super-hot during the day, too hot to write, probably would have smeared the ink with sweat.

By the time I got up this morning, Dad was out somewhere. I figured Becky was at Carol's with Evie, trying to clear out the pool at her condo complex. The sound of chain saws finally got me out of bed. I had my tea alone on the front porch where I watched one guy cut and bag fallen branches and palms from the library property across the street. Three other guys sat on the steps and watched. All wore white shirts that read PUBLIC WORKS on the back and drank from Styrofoam cups full of what could only have been café con leche.

I went back to work at Gil's for a couple of hours this evening. Mike pulled one of the big trucks to the front of the store to block the sun. They had a generator to run portions of the AC and some of the coolers inside. You still couldn't move too fast without working up a sweat. But I wanted to be there. I wanted to see if Mike would walk home with me after closing. He'd done it a few times before the storm if we were leaving at the same time. So I waited while he locked the doors. He didn't say anything about me waiting, or about seeing me during the eye of the storm.

"Gil said the National Guard should be here soon with water, food and dry ice."

We walked down the street towards his corner. It was so much brighter—so many leaves, branches and big pieces of trees had come down. Many still lay on the sidewalk or piled into empty parking spots on the side of the street.

"My Dad isn't expecting any help. He thinks all government and military resources are occupied on the mainland, or in Latin America. And TJ says there's no word at the hospital about bringing back the evacuated patients, even after the power comes back."

Maybe they're starting to forget us, I thought.

We'd reached his corner. I looked at him, something I usually don't, or can't do. I thought of his hand over his heart and wanted to wipe the sweat from my forehead.

"See you tomorrow?" I asked. He looked at me and smiled.

"Sure thing, morning might be better, cooler."

That's how it is now, schedules are run by the sun. I write at night with a flashlight once it's dark just before going to bed. And, no one sleeps in a bed, we move from room to room, from couch to chair to piece of floor where the breeze is the strongest, even if that means outside on the back deck. Actually, outside is best, with no lights, and the moon only half full. Last night the sky was incredible, full of stars. I wondered if Mike saw them. Maybe I'll ask tomorrow.

Tuesday June 14

Still no National Guard. Still no power. A lot of grumbling around Gil's about lack of support. According to the trusty weather radio, it's been in the upper eighties during the day with a heat index near 100. This afternoon Becky and I washed clothes in a tub on the back deck. Dad and TJ had strung a clothesline. In the direct sun they dried as fast as in the electric dryer.

It's really quiet, even during the day, still no planes or AC units. Only a few cars and mopeds on the streets. At night the moon is getting bigger, starting to make shadows on the back deck. I fall asleep thinking about what Mike might be looking at out his window.

Wednesday June 15

Self-obsessed much? I haven't written anything about Evie. Not sure what to write, really. I have no experience with babies, but she's definitely not a "regular" baby either, and that is not a bad thing. She's quiet, like she has not made a sound since she came home.

Tonight, Becky and I were on the back porch, the dogs asleep under the table, a slight breeze blowing. Evie was in her usual spot—in a sling close to Becky's chest.

"Does she cry?" I asked.

"No," she said, and lowered her voice. "Josie, she hasn't even eaten, not a thing."

I thought she might be joking, or referring to some kind of breast feeding thing. "I saw you feeding her peas after the hurricane."

"Well, 'normal' new born babies would not eat peas. You saw me smushing up peas for her. I was desperate."

"Jesus, Becky, she's over a week old."

"I know that Josie," she looked down at Evie. "But look at her. She's okay, and growing. I haven't weighed her, but I know she's heavier." She put her hand under the sling and bounced her. Evie let out what sounded like a giggle.

I reached out and put my hand on top of her head. "Cool," I said.

"That too," Becky said. "She never feels warm, she actually keeps me cool at night." She grabbed my hand. "Don't say anything, please."

"Okay, but you think she's okay? Really."

She looked down at her again and Evie smiled. She reached her tiny hand to Becky's check.

"She's perfect." She said it quietly, like I wasn't there. She was speaking to Evie, her daughter.

I saw it, Becky was a mother.

———

Everything thought wrong with me, honored in Evie, so different.

Seeva relaxes and continues to read.

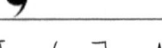

Thursday June 16

Power is back! There've been a lot of the big bucket trucks around, and Dad said all the properties he watches had it back yesterday, and Gil's too. Then early this morning the lights and ceiling fans turned on with the whir of central AC units around the neighborhood. It was a little weird—everything that had been on during the hurricane suddenly coming back to life. So the first thing we had to do was go around closing windows and doors and turning off lights.

Dad spent the day on the radio. He'd heard government officials have been performing different health checks at road blocks around South Florida, where the National Guard was after the hurricane. At the road block in Florida City Monroe County officials were checking IDs. Only those with a valid Florida ID with Monroe County address are getting through—after some type of blood test. And TJ said it's official, none of the patients that were evacuated from the hospital are being brought back.

It's so weird hearing about all this while the lights are back on and work was pretty normal today, although the credit card machines still weren't working.

Sunday June 19

Okay, there's another one called Earl. Tropical Storm *Earl*? Seriously? What a stupid name.

I worked this morning. It's pretty much back to usual, but there's only me, Gil, Mike, Pam, and Doug—a bagger who says he started working there when he was my age, which I guess was 30 to 50 years ago? It's hard to tell. Mike seemed distracted, not smiling much. Pam told me he hasn't heard from his mom in a while. I hadn't thought about the fact that she might be up there, in Naples, alone. I want to let him know he can talk to me. But how much comfort can I offer to someone worrying about a mother?

Monday June 20

The news goes on. It's been a long time since we saw a mainland newspaper, but here's the latest headline from *The South Florida Times*:

Congress Must Fully Fund Battle Against O-meg and Swine Flu

I worked the day shift and was home early so I showed the paper to Dad.

"Considering what we now know about Evie, is this really such a big deal anymore?" I asked.

He sat at the table looking at a circuit board with long wires coming out of it.

"Solar panels soon to come!" he exclaimed.

I tapped the newspaper, pointing at the headline.

"I saw it," he said. "Yes, I think it's still a big deal, for those medical and governmental types." He put down the circuit board and looked at me. "We got very lucky when Evie was born. Sneaking into the emergency room in all of the evacuation chaos, then Hurricane Danielle hitting. I'll bet no one from the high school even remembers Becky was pregnant, or that she was asked to leave." He picked up a small screwdriver.

"I know," I said, remembering the other girls, Sasha and her friends who seemed to disappear. "So, we're okay down here?"

"We're not going anywhere. Let the rest of the state do what it thinks it needs to do." He looked up at me and smiled. "We're good."

I bent and kissed the top of his head, there were grey hairs mixed in with the brown curls. "Thanks, Dad."

True, I had no concept of a mother to worry about, or one who worried about me, but this I knew—the feeling of comfort from my Dad. All thoughts of leaving were gone. This was where I needed to be.

Tuesday June 21

This afternoon, Becky and I walked down to the Southern-most Point. There was no one on Whitehead Street, like no people, cars or scooters. The sidewalk and parking spaces were full of broken branches, dead leaves, and even some street signs and lights. We walked down the middle of the street because it was easier. The dogs were off leash and ran from pile to pile sniffing and peeing on everything. With so many trees gone or branches down there was hardly any shade, I felt exposed and could not stop squinting.

We passed the Green Parrot Bar, open with the fans churning and juke box playing some guitar heavy blues. Looking in as we passed, there were three guys in faded fishing shirts sitting at the corner of the bar.

"Nice to know some things stay the same no matter evacuations, hurricanes, or viruses," I said.

Most of the other businesses were still closed up with hurricane shutters or boarded up windows. The two story Victorian style house that served as a tourist trolley stop on the next corner was still empty. Carts, tables and chairs pulled in a group close to the house, all chained together, windows and doors still shuttered.

"You know the town is slow if the tourist trains aren't running," Becky said, looking down at Evie.

"Power is back on. I'm sure they'll be open soon and beckoning the cruise ships."

Becky groaned while smiling at Evie. "Maybe that rumored quarantine isn't such a bad thing? What do you think Miss Evelyn?" Becky bounced the sling on her chest.

We passed a house boarded up with plywood, *Damn You Danielle!* spray painted across the piece to the left of the front door. There was still a seaweed line as far as United Street and sand covering much of the street for the remaining block. It smelled like low tide baked in the sun. We didn't stay long. The side of the Southernmost Point marker that faced the sea had been sandblasted down to its concrete finish.

"Next time let's do this early in the morning," Becky said.

We were both sweating, a drop slid down my spine, my light blue tank top was dark with sweat over my belly.

"Good idea." I reached over and touched Evie's cheek, still cool with no sign of sunburn on her light café con leche skin. She turned to look at me her hazel eyes clear and open. I felt cooler, relaxed and smiled back, rubbing my fingers lightly over her soft cheek.

Wednesday June 22

Earl spared us—stayed out in the Gulf swirling around until it finally just spun itself out.

I guess power is back on all over the island now. Talk at the store is that a lot of the people who evacuated and then met road blocks trying to get back have decided to stay on the mainland. Especially those who rented and worked in a restaurant or bar that closed for the storm.

Also since the storm, Internet and cell service are gone. Mike helped a woman put up two bulletin boards out front for notices—things for sale, help wanted, and apartments for rent. And, with so many evacuations, then the issue getting back in, and no cell service or Internet, there were even a few "have you seen" notices. Mike had my Dad rig the pay phone out front so you don't have to pay but it does time out after five minutes. It's nice that people have some way to let others know we're still here.

Thursday June 23

Carol told us this morning while we were sitting on the back deck that Becky's mom was leaving. Becky had Evie on a blanket under speckled shade from the Royal Poinciana tree branch hanging over the fence from the neighbor's yard. A lot of branches fell during the storm but leaves have already sprouted. Not that Evie seemed to mind being in the sun—she never even squinted.

"Hey," I said. "Maybe she's going to the Olympics!" I held up today's *South Florida Times:*

Come to the Olympics in Brazil – O-meg is Under Control

Becky laughed and tickled Evie's feet. Evie giggled. "She always goes away during the summer, to conferences and stuff."

Carol put down her knitting, another odd shaped purple bundle of yarn. "She's not coming back. She said all the storms so far have unnerved her."

Becky busied herself with Evie's toes as she kicked and giggled, a quiet, even sound.

"She used that word, *unnerved*, didn't she?" I asked.

Becky and Carol said "Of course she did," at the same time. They looked at each other and Carol shook her head with a sigh.

"Anyone want some iced tea?" I asked.

"Yes, and an ice cube for Evie," Becky said. "She keeps puckering her face and her gums feel warm."

She can't be teething already, I thought but didn't say anything. From the kitchen, I could hear Carol and Becky talking. Becky's mother was leaving. I still hadn't written back to my mother, didn't have a chance to think about it really—what did I have to say?

Sunday June 26

"My mom left this morning," Becky said.

We were in the bathroom, she was giving Evie a bath. The plastic shower curtain was flipped over the rod. Becky sat on the edge of the tub. I kneeled on a towel on the floor.

"Did you see her?" I asked, swirling my hands in the water. Evie watched the ripples. Three weeks old and she was sitting up in the shallow water.

"Nope," she dipped a cup in the water and dribbled it over Evie's tiny head. She turned her face so the water dripped onto her forehead.

"According to Carol she's going up to Cape Coral. Thinks she'll be safe there."

"Right," I said. "Ms. Paranoid is going up to the main-land—to virus central if you believe the news, and thinks she'll be safe?" I stood and put the toilet lid down to sit on.

"I doubt she'll feel safe until she reaches the dry, high mountains of Colorado."

"Did she ask about Evie?" I got a thick red towel from the shelf above the toilet. We'd always had nice towels from one of the snowbirds' houses that Dad took care of. Most were the type of people who liked to replace such things every season. Evie looked at me, and a drop of water ran over her right eye. She smiled, lips just a shade darker than her skin.

"You know what?" Becky said. "I didn't ask. I don't care. Evie is going to be surrounded by nothing but love if I have any-thing to do with it and I don't think that woman is capable of love."

At that point Evie kicked her legs.

"My little swimmer," Becky said and tickled the bottom of her feet. She kicked again like a frog.

———

Seeva, sitting on damp, warped linoleum, smiles at the thought of open water, legs stretching, toes wiggling.

Not now.

Thunder grows louder, clouds darken the horizon, Cloyal still searches, Seeva still reads. Both discovering.

Tuesday June 28

Things are pretty much back to normal. The town is less shady and less crowded but the news goes on. I brought both papers home from work to show Becky.

Headline from *The South Florida Times:*

First Baby Born with O-meg Related Birth Defects Born in Florida

And *The Key West News:*

No O-meg Reported in Key West

"You have to admit, these are funny, considering," I said. "I guess it's more like 'creative non-fiction' that we learned about in AP English."

"Yeah, I laugh and feel lucky." She held Evie out to me. We were sitting on the front porch, the sky darkening after sunset. I wrapped my hands gently around Evie's narrow chest and sat her on my knee. She was light, like a bunch of bananas, and cool to the touch, but not cold.

"Has she eaten anything yet?"

"Oh yeah," she said. "Smile for Auntie."

Evie turned and smiled at me, showing tiny straight teeth.

"Maybe some birth 'differences,' but no defects here."

Not knowing anything about babies, I wasn't sure how to react. So I just smiled back.

Thursday June 30

Dad was in the kitchen this morning, humming.

"Why?" I asked, as I put the kettle on for tea. "Why are you humming!?" I slumped down at the table and looked at the paper.

He sang out in a gravelly voice, "I need a hero!"

"Oh my god," I lay my head down after seeing the headline

from *The South Florida Times:*

Suarez Can Be a Hero in the O-meg Fight

"Governor Suarez to the rescue?" I said into my folded arms. "That might be scarier than any virus or genetically modified insects."

He laughed and kissed the top of my head as he went by. He still spends his day caring for all the properties he's responsible for, but I don't think those people will be coming back this season. The headlines, the radio stories, the politics—I think we've been forgotten.

Friday July 1

I saw *The South Florida Times* in the rack at work, headline:

Florida Confirms 10 New O-meg Cases Most in Single Day

A certain county? The entire state? They couldn't narrow it down a bit? We know it's not such a big deal but not sure who else knows. Who knew what was happening to all these new cases? These "cases" were people.

When I got home the house was empty. Becky's been spending a lot of time with Carol—because she has a pool at her condo, and no one else is around to use it. Sometimes I felt like I was chasing after Becky. I had no idea where Dad was, and even the dogs were gone, so I put on my swimsuit under a pair of shorts and headed out, tempted to take the long way by Gil's house but didn't.

And there they were, Becky and Carol sitting on the steps in the shallow end. Evie, with a water wing around her entire body, kicking between them. Pepper wagged her tail and Sargent raised his head to look at me but neither moved from their shady spot under a table.

Becky pointed at the newspaper on the table, opened to the health section.

Health–Cuba Boasts It Almost Eradicated O-meg

"We're betting on how long it'll take my mother to try and immigrate to Cuba. Want to join in?"

I slipped into the water and Becky lightly pushed Evie towards me. Under the shade of a bougainvillea blooming with white petals, I watched this tiny being, kicking and stroking, moving towards me as no 26 day old human could.

Sunday July 3

Tropical Storm Fiona, between Yucatan and Cuba headed north, forecast to miss us.

There was a note on the bulletin board for a *Reclaiming of Sunset Celebration* at Mallory Square tonight, a copy of the city seal at the top. Dad echoed my thoughts as he left to check it out.

"Not sure who we are reclaiming it from," he said before pedaling away on his bicycle.

I guess they're trying to get life back to normal, drawing in the tourists and such. But, really? There are no tourists. I didn't go. Becky didn't want any part of it either. She's still reluctant to take Evie out anywhere too public, especially considering O-meg is still in the news. When Dad came back he said we didn't miss anything.

"It was actually kind of sad," he told us. We sat out back watching the sky darken. "Some of the regular artists and performers I remember from the eighties, still trying to make a go of it, but there was no one there. I didn't stay long. I just couldn't."

I don't think this is the time for anyone to be thinking of vacations or celebrations, especially in Florida.

Monday July 4

Happy Independence Day…? So much for a holiday weekend. Maybe the storm kept everyone away? Fiona headed for Alabama, away from us. The tourists stayed away too. A lot of guest houses are still boarded up from Danielle. This should've been a big weekend with the 4th falling on a Monday, but the town is empty, it's eerie, but also nice?

Sunday was quiet at Gil's so Mike told us at the end of the day, after he'd locked the door and we were running the final receipts on the registers, that we could have Monday off.

"I'll come in for a few hours, but I'm not expecting anything, probably close by noon."

"What about Gil?" I asked as I gave him my cash drawer. He lowered his voice and walked backwards into the office, putting my drawer down on the counter.

"I can't get him away from the TV, and we only get two channels, both national news out of Miami. I almost wish the electricity was still out."

"Hey," I put my hand on the counter close to his. "Did you ever hear from your mom?"

"Yeah, she sounded really tired. I guess things are weird in Naples, no one wants to leave their house, afraid of mosquitos. Gil was on the phone for a long time with her." He looked down and started putting the loose quarters on the counter. "That's when he started watching so much TV."

I looked up when Mike put on his work smile for Pam standing behind me.

"Thanks, Pam, have a great day off."

"You bet," she rasped, pulling a red pack of More cigarettes out of her purse. "I'm gonna turn the AC so far down icicles form on the window sills."

I waited to see if he would put the drawers in the safe and come out of the office but he started to count the quarters, so I walked out with Pam.

No big fireworks tonight, not even any bottle rockets in the neighborhood. Dad, Carol, TJ and Becky spent the evening playing poker, using toothpicks as money. Evie sat on Becky's lap watching. I took Pepper out for a walk, but Sargent stayed under the table close to Becky, licking Evie's feet occasionally making her giggle and kick.

On the way home with Pepper, I walked by Gil's house, slowly. The only movement I saw was the blue flickering light of a television through the curtains. Pepper sniffed what was left of the tree that had fallen on the house across the street. I let her sniff a long time as I strained to see Mike's cottage through the bushes beyond the driveway. It looked dark.

Tuesday July 5

Another letter. I got this one out of the mailbox, the post-mark is almost a month old

Dear Josie,
I'm worried. There're grumblings up here in "America" (as

your Dad used to call it.) People are taking this virus seriously. Some people think the news isn't reporting all the cases. No one seems to know what the symptoms are, and some of the radical politicians are calling for the borders of Florida to be closed. Would you come to me if asked? Would you come if you could still get out of the state? I never heard from you after your birthday. Maybe I shouldn't expect to. I have a feeling you wouldn't leave your Dad, and I know he's not willing to leave that island. I'll comfort myself knowing he'll do everything in his power to keep you safe. And if anyone can survive any kind of disaster down there, it's your father.

All of my love,

Mom

I'm kind of pissed. Really? Over 10 years later and she thinks I would go to *her* in the case of an emergency, when the state seems to be falling apart? Shit, I feel guilty for even thinking I wanted to leave to try and find her a few months ago.

I'm not showing anyone this letter.

Wednesday July 6

According to *The South Florida Times:* 11 cases in one day. That's how it was printed, nothing about what type of cases. Nothing else about any O-meg babies being born on the mainland. I don't like to think about how they and their mothers might be treated, and I definitely don't bring it up to Becky. Even though, with Evie being just over a month old, we know, at this point, this "virus" hasn't shown up in any negative ways, or if it even is a virus.

Also, we don't know how she will grow and change. In other words there are still a lot of unknowns.

So Fiona hit Alabama as a Category 1. The weird thing is—it didn't weaken. Dad heard on his radio it still had 90 mile per hour winds as it headed toward Northern Georgia. They were talking about it when I came down from showering after work. It'd been super slow, so I dusted and faced shelves for, like, hours.

Everyone was on the back deck. The sky changed from a hot light blue to a cool dark indigo. Becky and Dad played cards. Sargent was curled around Evie—she lay with her head propped on his belly. I grabbed the dog brush from the table by the back door and started to brush Pepper. Evie's eyes moved as she watched a butterfly dipping in and out of the lime tree. Carol sat at the table, knitting and cursing softly under her breath as she tried to count her stitches. Carol's curses had recently turned to "poop," "shoot," or "phooey."

"Nothing normal about this hurricane season," Dad said. He shook the hair out of his eyes.

"Hey, you know Becky can cut hair. She takes care of mine." I rubbed my hand across my own short locks. "Not that there's much to take care of."

"We'll see, short or long, I don't really notice." He rearranged the cards in his hand. Becky slapped her hand of cards on the table.

"Gin," she said with a big smile. "Don't worry, Robbie, I'll just add that and the cost of a haircut to your tab."

Carol laughed. Evie turned from the butterfly and smiled at Dad.

"You girls are a laugh riot," he said.

Laying my head against the back of the plastic deck chair, I kept my hand on Pepper's warm back and listened to the sounds of their laughter. I felt okay—safe, home.

This is where I need to be.

Friday July 8

Dad was on the radio last night with someone from South Carolina. Fiona churned through and hit North Carolina still as a Category 1 hurricane yesterday.

Saturday July 9

The fun never stops…another storm…in the Atlantic. I tried not thinking about it, but the chatter at the store was heavy today. Constant stream of people buying hurricane supplies, again. Lots of talk about not evacuating after the nightmare some people went through trying to get back home after Danielle. Plus there are people who left that no one has heard from. There's also rumblings about some kind of quarantine imposed by the Governor, kind of like what my mother wrote about.

"Just gonna ride it out," one old leathery guy told me as he bought eighteen cans of tuna and four twelve packs of beer. "Maybe I'll evacuate after the storm when the power is out for over a week!" He laughed, revealing empty gums in the bottom of his mouth.

He'll tough it out and survive, where else could he go?

Tuesday July 12

Forecast not looking good. Gaston, a strong Category 1 hurricane with 90 mile per hour winds, now below Cuba, forecast to swing into the Gulf, then take a turn for us.

More people in the store buying supplies, opting to ride this one out rather than evacuate. A ton of bottled water and canned goods came through my register. I think I'm getting biceps!

Dad and TJ got the houses ready, again. Dad was grumbling about solar panels, he never got them hooked up. TJ's been hanging around a lot because the hospital never fully reopened after Danielle, just the emergency room, so no big evacuation effort for patients this time.

I wanted to ask Mike how Gil was doing, but he was running around the store bagging and restocking on his own. I guess Gil was at home.

Thursday July 14

The weather people predicted this one right. Gaston strengthened and turned towards the Keys. Because of the tides and the moon, they predicted a big tidal surge—eight to ten feet. We'll be fine, relatively speaking, living on the highest part of the island, all eighteen feet of it.

Police cars drove the streets announcing the mandatory evacuation of all residents and suspension of all emergency services. In other words, we're really on our own for this one. It feels a little creepy but I don't let myself dwell. Everyone is here, so here is where I feel safe.

Hurricane Gaston started yesterday afternoon around two o'clock. Gaston seemed stormier than Danielle. We were back in the living room, TJ was with us this time. Figuring the power would go out, Carol had been here for two days. She lay back in a recliner in the corner, eyes on the ceiling where the fan moved slowly in gusts of warm wind that found a way in through the closed shutters. Rain sometimes made it in with the wind. I guess it was too damp to knit.

No card games this time. Dad and TJ talked about growing up on the island. In the 80s, the town was so quiet during the off season, they would race their bikes down the middle of Duval Street in July. They could fish off Mallory Square pier, then quietly applaud the setting sun with the few other locals who stopped by to watch.

"That's what I wanted to reclaim about sunset last week," Dad said quietly. (Well it sounded quiet amongst the rain and wind from outside.) He continued, "But they still want it to be all about the tourists."

TJ added, "Everyone's so scared. I wonder what it would take to bring tourists back."

Sometimes it was hard to hear them over the howl of the wind or whip of the palms and branches on the roof. I still took comfort in the tone and cadence of their voices. Becky and I lay with our heads at opposite ends of the couch, Evie crawled over our tangled legs. The light pressure of her small cool palms was almost unnoticeable. Sargent and Pepper curled together under Carol's propped up recliner. No one had turned on the weather radio. As Dad and TJ ran out of stories, we listened to Mother Nature whip and howl outside. It was hard to sleep. Nothing sounds quite like hard rain on a tin roof, no matter how good the insulation is. At least most of the neighbor's Spanish limes came down during the last storm.

Sunday July 17

Gaston finished with the wind and rain this morning, but the worst came after. We finally turned on the weather radio to hear that a reported storm surge of eight feet had pushed through from the Gulf and hit the island with nowhere to go.

A friend of Carol's called on the land line in the afternoon. She lives down by the cemetery in an old wooden conch house. They'd evacuated to the county detention center on Stock Island where her husband worked as a guard. She said Stock Island was flooded, water up to the roofs of cars in the parking lot. She'd been trying to call friends in New Town, but no one answered.

Dad and TJ took a walk down to the end of our street. Dad said there was a debris line of broken branches, leaves, and garbage just past Frances Street, like the high tide mark of seaweed on a beach. He wanted us all to stay in until tomorrow. I spent the afternoon by the window in the front room watching to see if Mike walked by. No one bothered me. Everyone else was at the table playing Gin. Evie crawled over and pulled herself up into my lap. Her cool skin felt good against my bare legs. The shutters were open, the wind was warm and humid.

The large buttonwood tree next to the library across the street had lost a huge branch, about twenty feet long. Tangled with power lines, it filled the sidewalk and two parking spaces. The tree looked lopsided. Remembering the one guy taking care of the debris after the last storm while the others sat on the steps and drank coffee, I wondered if there were any county workers left in town to take care of this new round of debris. If the flooding was as bad as it sounded, I wondered who would be able to stay on the island, or who would want to anymore.

Evie sat sideways on my lap, leaning against my stomach, swinging her short legs. *My Little Swimmer* Becky had called her.

Monday July 18

Cleaning up, again. I can't believe there were still branches and leaves left to come down. Before starting the sweeping, raking and bagging, we walked around the neighborhood. The paradise olive tree on the corner fell down, but not before the lashing wind and rain coated the white house a burnt orange color.

After two blocks TJ spoke up, "No more For Sale signs. Blown away or giving up. Something tells me we won't see many of those for a while." He kicked a coconut laying by the curb.

I looked around. "I don't think there are any coconut trees on this block."

"Doesn't look much like paradise anymore," Becky said. She held Evie on her hip. She wore a baby sized tie dyed t-shirt, long enough to be a dress, and looked intently towards the end of the street in the direction Dad had mentioned seeing the high water mark yesterday, her legs swinging.

Tuesday July 19

The news goes on! I saw yesterday's mainland paper at

Gil's today. I wasn't sure if Mike would open. I just happened to be walking by…there was a bundle of *The South Florida Times* by the doors. I knocked when I saw him walk by the registers with a broom.

He opened the door to pick up the bundle of newspapers. "That guy is amazing, like the post office, he delivers the newspapers rain or shine, or hurricanes or floods apparently." He smiled. He wore a UCF tank top, long jean cutoffs and rubber flip flops. "Hey, I was hoping to see you."

I tried to breathe normally. We stood in the open sliding doors. The inside of the store was sweltering.

"Do you want to come in tomorrow? Just a few hours first thing in the morning before it gets too hot. I've been checking for any damage or leaks and I think we're good. I just need to make sure the generator works." The ends of his hair were dark with sweat. I wiped my forehead with the back of my hand.

"Sure," I said, hoping it sounded off handed enough. Inside I was all *yes yes yes*!

He fanned himself with a small brown paper bag. "I know it's disgustingly hot, so I have a plan to set up out in front and only come in when someone needs something. The walk-in stayed cold even after the power went out. So I'll move everything into the closed cooler and then get the generator going."

He stopped talking and looked at me. Those eyes. I swallowed and pointed at the newspaper headline:

An O-meg Mystery – How Did a Utah Man Contract Virus

"You know I don't think this O-meg thing is that big of a deal," I said. Why was I still nervous around him?

"Probably not," he lifted the papers to his chest. "It seems like they're trying to distract us from something else. Too many articles about what might happen instead of what has happened."

As I walked home, I wondered what he would think of Evie.

Wednesday July 20

Back to work, kind of. No power of course, so the generator rumbled. Still a bit stuffy, so Mike only let customers in a few at a time, and kept the coolers locked. He got Gil to come in for the first hour and help restock the shelves after the craziness of all the hurricane supply shopping. I saw him in the aisles.

"There's still a foot of water in parts of New Town," a stooped gray haired woman told Gil in front of the canned beans.

"There was four feet of water over the airport tarmac on Sunday afternoon," Gil added, running a white hankie over his bald head.

"Hospital flooded, too," a thin man with dread locks and no shirt said. "No word if either of them will reopen."

I watched Gil nod and go back to stocking cans of evaporated milk. It looked like his hands shook.

Mike closed by noon before it got too hot. Becky showed up with Evie wrapped in a light blanket. I had no idea she felt comfortable bringing Evie out in public yet. She walked over to the office with me as I returned the key for the coolers. Mike looked at me smiling, then noticed Becky behind me. He glanced at Evie.

"Cute," he said with a small smile. He looked embarrassed. "Sorry, I'm not much of a kid person—only child, not even any cousins."

Becky laughed. "No problem—she's not your usual kid."

He took the key from my hand. I held it so that our fingers touched, then felt my face go warm. I fanned my hand in front of my face as if the heat in the store bothered me.

"Maybe tomorrow will be cooler."

"Maybe," he said. "So, see you tomorrow?"

"Okay," I said and looked at his face, stubbled with brown hairs. He had no reaction to Evie.

"Great," he said.

And I really wanted to touch him, maybe his hand that held the key or his forearm. I wanted him to know something. I wanted to share something with him. Instead I followed Becky out of the store.

She didn't even tease me on the way home. The sun was high, so I squinted behind my sunglasses not sure what to say about Mike, or about her bringing Evie out.

At the house she kept walking. "We're going swimming," she said and headed down the street towards Carol's pool. I didn't want to go, but she also didn't invite me. I guess I didn't need inviting. A cloud moved over the sun and I took a moment to enjoy a few seconds of shade.

Thursday July 21

Gil was at the store this morning. He said more people were trying to leave since their houses got flooded. He stood by the front door talking with an old man who came in everyday for a can of soda. Gil said something about maybe wanting to take chances on the mainland with mosquitos and quarantines.

"And those rumors can't be true—about men being rounded up or just disappearing at night? Doesn't make sense, that
wouldn't happen in this country," his voice rose.

Mike brought the old man a can of root beer. "On the
house, Mr. Bauer, we're closing early today," he said and pulled Gil
towards the office. He didn't resist.

I could just make out Mike's voice in the office. I didn't
know what to do, so I wiped down the register areas. Pam went
outside to smoke.

Five minutes later Mike came over to me. He touched my
back. I wanted to lean into him.

"I'm closing early again. It's hot, and the generator is acting
up. No one's thinking straight. I wish it would rain soon, cool it
off, wash some of the dust away." His hand was now flat on my
back and I did lean a little. "I'll see you tomorrow," he said and
walked back to the office.

I liked that he said it as a statement, not a question.

Friday July 22

Still no power, but maybe soon? The marine store was open
and Dad got the deep cycle batteries and wiring for our solar panels. He spun me around the kitchen singing, "Fans and lights, and
ice, oh my!"

It felt good to swing around with Dad, both laughing as
we twirled. It felt like I hadn't seen him in days. Everything felt
different, like Mike, like Evie. I feared life would never go back to
anything called normal, but back to semi-normal would be okay.

I think Becky's given up on Dave.

I was gathering dish towels to wash on the back deck when Dad brought in the paper and tossed it on the table. She was feeding Evie oatmeal and looked at the paper. Evie had to grab the spoon and direct it towards her mouth, because Becky was getting ready to put it in her ear.

Headline from *The South Florida Times:*

Colombia Declares Much-Feared O-meg Crisis Over as Infection Rate Plummets

Dad wiped Evie's cheek, and it looked like she mouthed the word "thanks." I don't think he noticed.

"They're just trying to bolster confidence for people heading to the area for the Olympics," he said.

She sat Evie in the chair and took the bowl to the sink. "Whatever," she said. "Go USA." And pumped her fist.

The Olympics? I can't imagine life for some is still *that* normal. I waited to see if Becky said anything else. She just scooped up Evie and left.

Monday July 25

How nice, it was *only* a tropical depression that rolled through last night. A lot of rain, just enough to top off the rain barrels and cool off the house. Still no power.

Becky had been around the house all day, fiddling with the manual sewing machine. I moved about the house with a book (ugh, *Moby Dick* at my Dad's suggestion/insistence), changing positions as the shade and breeze direction changed. Just before sunset, we both sat on the front porch with Evie. The clouds were just starting to blow in. Evie stood, holding onto Becky's chair. Looking out onto the street a rooster chased a chicken across the road. The hen got away in the dead branches still covering the sidewalk in front of the library. Other than the caws and squawks of the birds it was quiet. It felt ghostly, more like late September, the slowest of the slow part of the year.

"I have the feeling this is how it's going to be from now on." I went out to the middle of the street and looked in both directions. "No cars, no scooters, of course most of those were lost in Gaston, but I don't even see anyone on a bicycle. Just us and the chickens." The stray tabby cat that lived around the library shot across the street. "And the cats."

I skipped steps back up to the porch. Becky held up Evie as she stood. When Becky took her hands away Evie still stood, she didn't sway.

"How tall is she?" I asked.

"Twenty three inches. What if I started marking her height on the bathroom door jamb?"

"It's your house too Becky, you don't have to ask."

Becky held Evie's hands as she slowly twirled around. "Our marks are still there. Remember when your Dad started marking our heights?"

I did. It was right after my mother left but I didn't say anything. I hadn't told her about the second letter, I wanted to ignore it.

"What do you make of all this?" I asked as Evie took a small step towards me. She wore another tie dye shirt, this one with a heart on the front. I didn't know what I was referring to, I felt like I hadn't talked to Becky in weeks.

"I don't know, it's not like I have anything to compare her with. This is way beyond *What to Expect The first Two Years.*" She scooped up Evie and cuddled her, kissing her nose repeatedly while she cooed with laughter, like a quiet melody.

I guess I didn't know what to expect any more either. Whatever it might be, Becky and Evie were in it together.

Wednesday July 27

Nothing out of the ordinary other than work, sweat, loud generators and cool showers on the back deck. Dad installed an outdoor shower with a solar hot water heater on the roof of the shed. But who wants a hot shower now? Heat index is easily over 100 during the days. At this point I wonder if Key West will ever get electricity back. New Town is toast, soggy toast. Maybe they can get power back to Old Town eventually. Who knows? Who knows anything at this point?

Thursday July 28

I hadn't seen Becky in a couple of days, since we talked on the front porch that night. Naturally, she spends all her time with Evie so it's not like I'm being ignored. I'm at work most days anyway, if you can call it that. I go in everyday just to be around Mike. Pam is there too. It's like we don't know what else to do with ourselves.

When I heard Becky come in just before sunset, I was on the floor on the other side of my bed, reading. I didn't get up. Her door creaked as she pushed it halfway closed. A breeze blew in through the open windows, rooms and hallway. Later, the screen door slammed and Dad and TJ's voices drifted up. Since Gaston drastically reduced the livable portions of the island, they'd been riding bikes around at sunset, "seeing and being seen" is what Dad says, but it seems like they're on patrol.

A chair scraped across the wood floor. I'd been alone the entire afternoon and had no desire to be seen, so instead of going down, I moved to the top of the stairs to listen.

"I don't think anyone is paying attention to anything past First Avenue. Electricity, trash pickup, there's nothing going on," Dad said. "I rode around with one of the landscapers from the Hudson property. Some streets past Fifth aren't even passable because of downed trees, power lines or odd household items that floated out of destroyed houses."

TJ continued, "Most places out there are unlivable. With no power, the mold sets in. One of the guys I used to work with lived on Northside Drive. He only had six inches of water over his floors and considered himself lucky that it didn't get into the electrical outlets. But now the baseboards are swollen and turning green."

"Soon to be black mold," Dad added.

"Yep, he's taking his chances and heading north in a few days."

"Really."

I could hear the questioning in Dad's voice and pictured him leaning back to look at the stained glass lamp that hung over the table. That's how he thought, by looking up.

"What do you think about that?" he asked.

It was so quiet, I could hear TJ sigh. "I don't know, Robbie. I feel okay here. It's our home. I know what to expect. I know the people who are left. I know how to live here. But up there." I pictured TJ waving towards the north. "Between crazy newspaper stories and paranoid TV news out of Miami, you couldn't pay me to leave Key West right now. But what about you? What about Josie? What about all the girls?"

"I have to keep telling myself they'll be fine, that we'll all be fine. That I can take care of them, no matter what. I know I can do that here. From what I've heard, I might not be able to do that up there."

"We all have to take care," TJ said.

"I know, I know. First, Evie and now all these storms… everything seems to be changing, and fast. I'm trying to keep up, to make life as normal as possible." He paused, "Whatever that means."

I didn't hear anything for a moment.

"You have three growing girls in this house," TJ started.

"No, no don't let Josie hear you say that. There are two young women and one growing girl in this house."

"Ah yes, Ms. JJ, not so Junior anymore. Are you ever going to let her help you? She can handle it. She hasn't freaked out about any of this, Becky, Evie, working, and preparing for hurricane after hurricane."

"Have you ever known Josie to freak out? Her mother left when she was barely six. And she never cried, as far as I knew. Just accepted her absence. She hasn't even said anything about the birthday letter."

"Well, I've told you enough times that you deserve a lot of

the credit for that calm disposition, you never gave her the time to miss her mother or freak out. And, you could have freaked about the letter, too."

"My days of freaking out over that woman are long gone. I got the best gift in my life when she left. Now, I just have to take care of Josie while the entire world changes."

Then I heard Dad sigh.

"We all take care of each other, brother."

My stomach felt hollow. Two brothers downstairs, Becky and Evie in the room across the hall, and me in between. All a family, so why did I feel alone? I heard the flick of a lighter and the floor at the bottom of the stairs glowed in candlelight. I hadn't realized it was dark.

———

A flash and a crack of thunder draws Seeva's attention away from the notebook. The sky is slate gray, Seeva hears waves breaking against the building's foundation. The air through the windows is wet. Seeva shivers, hoping the storm passes quickly, wanting the sun to return.

Feeling for Cloyal, concentrating, against the chill in the wind's growing intensity.

Cloyal?

Waits. Rain drops heavy. Waves break. Wind builds.

Safe, Seeva feels, as the gale begins.

Tuesday August 2

Well hello, and goodbye Hermine! A blustery couple of days was actually Tropical Storm Hermine rolling around in the Gulf before cutting through the southern part of the state and briefly gaining hurricane strength over Lake Okeechobee. Hurricanes that travel and strengthen over land, how new and exciting is that!?

Also, exciting—electricity is back on, sort of, only in Old Town. Still a lot of brown outs in the afternoons, but today it stayed on all day, at the store and at home. Ah, air conditioning...

Wednesday August 3

Today Dad came home with a gun.

"I want to have one so we won't need one," he told us over dinner. "A Murphy's Law kind of thing."

"Where'd you get it?" I asked, staring at the gun, not looking at him.

"Don't worry about that."

"Fine." I pushed away from the table my chair legs scrapping loudly over the floor sticky with dried humidity after so long with no AC. Maybe I'd mop tomorrow.

"Come on, Josie. You two need to know how to load it." He let me handle it, the gun, first. Evie watched the whole time as we loaded and unloaded it. Then he put it on top of the bookcase in the living room. I can reach it standing on tip toe, but Becky would need to stand on a chair. He put the bullets in a glass flour container on top of the fridge.

So now we have a gun.

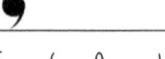

Celebratory dinner at TJ's tonight—solar panels on both houses now installed. And, I invited Mike at the last minute. It was just us at closing. Since the power was back he's been keeping the store open until sunset. As he locked the door I think I just blurted, "Want to come over to my Uncle's for dinner?" It's a blur but I remember him smiling and accepting. The walk over was nice, just a car and a couple of scooters went by and a few air conditioners hummed. It almost felt like a normal, slow, quiet summer evening.

TJ's front door was closed and the window AC unit rattled. His house has almost the exact lay out as ours, with the large open living room, dining room, kitchen combo, and what had been their parent's old bedroom on the first floor. TJ stood at the stove frying something in a wok. He'd gone out earlier and found some lobsters. Dad sat at the table looking at a chart, talking about laying crab traps in a couple of months. Carol was setting the table. A moment passed after Dad turned to us, then he held out his hand and said, "Well, hello, Mike."

Maybe it was just me but it felt like everyone stopped for a second before moving again. TJ offered him a beer. Becky looked over her shoulder and winked at me. She stood at the counter chopping broccoli, with Evie on a stool next to her. Evie is over two feet tall—I saw the mark on the door jam of the bathroom last night. She's starting to look like a skinny toddler.

Dinner conversation circled around hurricanes and headlines from the mainland. There hadn't been a local paper since the flooding and the mainland paper only showed up every few days. This was today's headline:

O-meg Concerns Could Disrupt Back-To-School Plans in Miami

"I read that one," Carol said with a wave of her hand. "Miami-Dade school officials are considering changing the time for the start of school so kids aren't waiting outside for the bus during heavy mosquito time." She shrugged and picked up her glass of wine. "Whatever time that is."

"I've heard parents are concerned about mosquitos on school grounds," Dad said. "So parents in rich neighborhoods are getting together to hire tutors and nannies to teach groups of the neighborhood kids."

"Well good for them if they can afford it," I said.

"Some families are trying to leave the state, or send their kids to out-of-state boarding schools," Mike added. Becky had made sure he sat next to me, and I could feel the timber of his voice in my chest as he continued. "But, Gil's been talking to my mom in Naples and it's no longer as simple as getting in a car or plane and leaving. Governor Suarez ordered checkpoints with blood tests on roads and in airports. No one is going anywhere until they've been tested for O-meg." For a moment no one said anything. Carol gave Evie a piece of broccoli.

"Right, because only Florida has mosquitos and O-meg," she said. "Did anyone read the article about the baby in Texas whose death was tied to O-meg?"

"I did," Becky rubbed the short soft strands of Evie's auburn hair. "What a crock. According to the hospital it looked like the baby died of SIDS, but when the father found her there was a mosquito in the room so he freaked out."

I elbowed her. "Wow, sounding like quite the expert."

She started collecting plates, so I stood to help. Mike took his plate to the sink and turned on the water. Becky winked at me again. *Helps in the kitchen, nice,* she mouthed.

"Whatever," she said with a smile. "I'm so over the O-meg drama." She handed me the plates and pushed me toward the sink. "Why don't you dry, Josie?"

"I think the fact that the hurricane season has taken on a sci-fi quality, there are other things to worry about," Dad said. He shuffled a deck of cards.

"So, Mike, Gil must be happy with all these storms? People having to stock up on hurricane supplies every two weeks?" TJ asked with a smile.

"I don't know. He's been pretty quiet lately. I think Gaston really threw him. All that water. He knows people who had four feet in their houses."

Dad shook his head. "I've heard that, too."

"Yeah, Uncle Gil has always been a big fan of boating and the ocean, he's the one who taught me how to sail and fish the back country. But he told me once the ocean comes into your home, that's it." He put the last bunch of silverware in the towel I held out. I smiled, I couldn't help it.

Later, we all walked the few blocks home together. Mike was with my Dad talking about Mike's mom. Carol, Becky and I lagged behind a few yards. Evie rode on Becky's shoulders. The night was warm, a breeze scented with night blooming jasmine kept it comfortable.

"It's nice, but also sad that it's this quiet," Carol said.

A scooter buzzed by, and a central AC unit rumbled on the other side of the street.

"There's still a few signs of normal Key West life," I said, bending to pick up a frangipani blossom off the sidewalk.

"Becky, darling, I didn't want to bring it up at dinner but did you see the other O-meg article in the paper?"

"The one about a bunch of U.S. troops having contracted the virus?"

"That answers my question," Carol said stopping to pat a skinny tabby cat.

"Did you read it?" I asked.

"He's been down there, somewhere, for over a year now. It's not that I've given up hope, but I'm not expecting any miracles either."

"But O-meg isn't that big of a deal, right?" I said.

"Maybe. But, I doubt any of the other medical people feel the same way. We have no idea what's happening out there to people who have the virus, or are born with it." She was rubbing Evie's shins, while holding her on her shoulders.

Dad and Mike had stopped in front of Gil's house. They shook hands.

"Thanks for having me over." Then he turned to me. "Thanks for inviting me, Josie."

My face heated up, and I was thankful for the dark. "No problem."

"I'll see you tomorrow." He reached over and tickled the bottom of Evie's foot. She kicked lightly and let out a soft hooting sound.

At the corner before heading to her condo, Carol bumped my arm.

"Becky's right. He's cute," she said and raised her eyebrows.

Behind me Becky snorted with laughter. With everything else going on, if I could stop blushing and acting so awkward around him, maybe the teasing would stop. But it was also nice to feel like I had Becky's attention again, and feel like I was included in a joke with her and Carol.

Friday August 5

I was buying a jar of macadamia nuts before going home when Mike brought up dinner the night before.

"Thanks again for having me over to your Uncle's for dinner."

Digging in my backpack for my money purse, I wasn't sure what to say, *sure, no problem, thank you for spending the evening with my crazy family...*

He rolled the jar back and forth between his hands.

"Evie," he started and I looked up. "She's kind of...different."

"She's very special to us."

"No, I know," he said looking at me, right in the eyes.

Don't blush, don't blush, I begged myself.

"I could tell. Do you want a bag for these?"

I couldn't' help it—I scoffed, "What do you think?" I pulled my backpack to my front and dropped in the jar.

"Right," he said with a smile. "So let me know if you do want to hang out again, or need help with Evie, or anything else." And, there it was, I felt my face go warm.

"Okay, yeah, great. See you tomorrow." I hoped I was moving in a straight line out the door. My knees were shaking.

Mike left the store early, said something about Gil and gave the keys to Pam. Not sure who, if anyone, would be at home and still wanting to believe life was normal, I picked up Chinese from the restaurant across the street. It's still open for take-out. When I got home Dad sat in a rocking chair on the front porch, rocking with his eyes closed. He opened them as I hit the first step.

"Look at you," he said with a smile. "Grown up and even providing food for your old man."

"Why do you think any of this is for you?"

The ends of his eyes sagged.

"Come on, I picked it up on my way home."

"Nice, that some things are still normal."

"What might pass for normal anyway," I said. "They're living in the restaurant, only open for pick-up. Their house on Patterson was flooded with over 2 feet of water for 3 days after Gaston."

Dad shook his head and took the warm bag of food from me as we walked into the house. The AC was just high enough to take the damp out of the air, and the ceiling fans were on high. Evie sat on the floor running her small hands down Pepper's back. Sargent slept under Becky's chair at the old manual sewing machine. Her foot pumped the lever at the bottom, making the needle move methodically over a piece of material. She'd finally gotten the hang of it a few weeks ago. She'd made curtains out of old sheets to keep out the sun but let in the breeze. I didn't know what she was making tonight.

It was just us for dinner. Evie sat on a pile of encyclopedias from 1998 eating the vegetables out of the Lo Mein. Halfway through the dumplings Dad stopped.

"I need to ask you two something. I want to make sure you're really okay staying here with everything that's going on." He looked up at the stained glass lamp that a local artist had made about ten years ago. He'd given it to my dad after an interview and photo spread in the paper.

"They may seem like conspiracy theories and craziness, but there is serious shit happening on the mainland and around the country. And we are pretty isolated here, for better and worse. I don't know what or who is left as far as law enforcement or government, and according to TJ the hospital was too damaged to reopen any time soon."

"Come on, Dad," I nudged his forearm. "This all sounds like a dream come true for you."

He smirked. "I know, but I worry about…"

Becky broke in. "I don't want to go anywhere. As long as you are okay with me and Evie being here, this is where I want to be."

"Ditto," I said, and knew it was true. I couldn't leave any of it…Dad, Becky, this half flooded island. I would never bring up my mother's second letter, and I would never respond. She made her choice all those years ago, and now I had made mine. I didn't need to find her. I had everything I needed here, always have.

"Okay," he said and gathered the empty containers for the garbage. "That's enough from me. I'll clean since you cooked, Josie."

"Awww, thanks, Dad."

He kissed the top of each of our heads on his way to the garbage pile out back.

Wednesday August 10

Mike didn't come in today. It was really a skeleton crew—no deli, no butcher, just Pam, Doug the bagger, and me. I spent a lot of time in the aisles, dusting, thinking about Dad, Evie, Becky, my family, and Mike, and the state, and the island, and…it was exhausting. I was exhausted.

When I got home I lay on the couch under the churning ceiling fan. Through the window I watched butterflies flit around the fruit trees. A giant iguana climbed down a palm tree and lay on the porch in the sun.

I dozed. Becky and Evie came in, talking quietly. A cool palm touched my cheek and I smiled in my half sleep. I felt better when they were home, when they were close. The coolness disappeared and I heard the front door shut. Alone again, my forehead tensed.

Thursday August 11

Mike watched me a lot at work, then asked me to stay until close. After he put my cash drawer in the safe, he asked how I was doing.

"I heard you were quiet yesterday," he added.

"Just tired," I said. "Tired of a lot of things." We were outside by this point. He locked the door.

"Not tired of here, I hope."

"No." I pointed at one of the signs taped on the inside of the glass. It was for a play at the Waterfront Theater from last March. That seemed like years ago. I wondered if the Waterfront would ever have plays again. After Gaston it may truly be a waterfront theater. I turned to look at him with a small smile. "Maybe I should get rid of these old posters tomorrow?"

"Let's get out of here," he said. He peered into the dark store, his unshaven face reflected back. "I mean, we live on an island, right?"

I looked into the reflection of his eyes in the window, they were shaded.

"I want to go to the beach. I want to get in the ocean." He turned to me. "When was the last time you even saw the ocean?"

"Yesterday, when I walked the dogs." I smiled.

He rolled his eyes. "Lucky you."

"But, wait," I actually grabbed his forearm. "That doesn't count. It was the ocean but it was covering the last three blocks of White Street." Letting go of his arm, I remembered how the wind from the Atlantic had blown small waves over the clear path of water left by the pavement. A white van had water up over the tires. The stop light at the intersection of Flagler hung down, one cable still attached to a street pole on the corner, the colored glass broken and the metal frame already covered with rust.

He took my wrist. "Come on, Gil's scooter is here. I'll drive—my treat."

We went to Ft. Zach. It was so close to sunset the ranger waved us in with a reminder we had fifteen minutes before they closed the park. I couldn't believe there were still rangers and the park was officially open. But his shirt was pretty wrinkled and he had quite a beard—maybe it wasn't so official after all. As we rode in we passed the police horse barn. It was empty but still smelled of horse and hay.

Mike pulled all the way in amongst the pines by the first

shower and locked my backpack and his wallet in the seat. It smelled good. It smelled just like Ft. Zach should—of pine and sea. We left our sneakers under a picnic table and tried to run but laughed and stumbled over the coral pieces close to the shore line. Mike dove as soon as his knees were under water. I waded up to my thighs before turning and falling back. My shorts and work polo felt heavy, but the water soaked into me like a warm salt bath. I closed my eyes and floated.

Mike popped up ten feet away and shook his head, hair flopped over one blue eye. I paddled out to where he treaded water. We faced the sea, away from the setting sun, rising and falling with the waves.

"There's another one out there," he said. I knew what he was talking about. Another storm in the Atlantic—Tropical Storm Ian—I'd heard people talking about it that day.

Mike dove a few more times. I paddled around on my back watching the orange sky deepen.

"I think we're close to our fifteen minutes." He treaded water about a foot away from me. I stayed on my back looking up at the fiery sky, not wanting to leave. I didn't want to go back to the house, hear the creepy weather radio voice and put a new mark on the tracking map.

We walked, dripping and cooled, to the scooter, carrying our shoes. On the ride over I'd been nervous and held onto more of his shirt than him. After the swim I was chilly and once again tired. As the sun set below the horizon the rainbow of the sky intensified and I wrapped my arms around his waist and held on. His back was warm even through our wet shirts. At the red light on Simonton Street he put his hand over mine until the light changed.

He dropped me in front of my house, saying nothing before shooting away. The sound of a scooter fading down the street was almost unfamiliar.

No one was home. I've given up trying to guess where the others might be. I rinsed off on the back deck in water warmed by the afternoon sun.

Saturday August 13

No *Key West News* since Gaston. Dad heard the office had four feet of water, everything ruined.

Oh, Tropical Storm Ian swirled away. Never got near us or anyone else. At the store today Mike wondered if we scared it away. It felt like a private joke between us. It was nice, and I don't think I blushed!

Monday August 15

Another storm rolled off the coast of Africa a few days ago, skipped disturbance and depression status and went right to a named tropical storm—Julia. It's pretty far north, no warnings or anything for the Caribbean. Good for us, probably not so good for the Northeast.

Tuesday August 16

According to our weather radio, Julia strengthened overnight into a hurricane, a really fast, very strong hurricane.

Tonight Becky and I took the dogs for a run around the cemetery. It was nice having her around. I haven't seen much of Carol since the power came back on. Evie, walking now, wasn't having any trouble keeping up, even with the dogs. She wore a little Gil's Groceries t-shirt. As we walked down Margaret Street, Becky told me about today's headlines from the mainland. That paper is still showing up every few days.

"Schools are distributing protective uniforms to students in O-meg zones. Can you believe it," she said. We unclipped the leashes at the entrance to the cemetery. The gates have been open since before the last storm. Technically, no dogs were allowed but no one was around to stop us. Sargent looked up at Becky then took off, and Pepper followed.

"I can just see all these little kids in child-sized yellow hazmat suits waiting for the bus, dropping from heat exhaustion," I groaned.

"But not getting bit by an evil diseased mosquito—that's the important thing," she added. "I am so glad to be down here." Evie, forever kicking off any shoes Becky tried to put on her, walked barefoot in the grass.

"It does scare me a little—if these are the things they are reporting, imagine what is NOT getting through." We stopped to sit on a bench. Sargent, barking close by, had probably found an iguana. Evie looked up at Becky.

"Go ahead." Evie gave a little squeak and ran towards the barking. She may look like a toddler but she moves like an adult without stumbling or staggering.

"I saw a story about a guy from Taiwan who vacationed

in Miami, then after returning home got worried, had a test and discovered he had O-meg. According to Dad's radio research the recent news is that the only ones who test positive for O-meg are men, and pregnant women."

"Scary," she said. "Especially after what your dad has heard about the Governor trying to quarantine all of South Florida. That type of story plays right into their fears."

"And what does that even mean, South Florida? It's not like there's a border. It's such a random distinction." A huge iguana moved down the trunk of a palm tree. It must have been four feet long, orange with thick black bands around the tail. I love iguanas—like small dinosaurs that roam the island. I was tempted to torture Becky, but didn't. They freak her out. She's been known to literally crawl over people in her haste to get away from them.

"I hope they just forget about us down here." Becky turned and whistled. Sargent gave a small half bark then ran from behind a crypt followed by Evie and Pepper.

"That wouldn't be such a bad thing," I agreed.

We stayed until it was dark, watching the full moon rise over a large banyan tree still standing near the Frances Street entrance. Walking home, I slowed as we passed through the fresh, sweet aroma of a Ylang-Ylang tree, and Evie placed her cool hand in mine.

Friday August 19

Yesterday Julia became a major hurricane—Category 4—145 mph winds, so big it looks like she'll take on the entire Northeast. All barrier islands from North Carolina to New York were ordered to evacuate. Dad talked to a guy from Manhattan on the radio. He said they're worried the tunnels will flood from the storm surge, so New York City closed the subways.

This season has gone catastrophic.

Saturday August 20

It's gotten much easier for me to talk with Mike since our beach visit, although there hasn't been anything else as nice as that. We still left the store together but he headed right for his house. I think he was worried about Gil, who hasn't been at the store since the power came back on weeks ago. And I don't know the last time he spoke to his mom.

How do I ask Mike about his mom? About his worries? How do I let him know I care?

Sunday August 21

Dad found a woman on the radio from New Jersey. She told him things were a mess. Julia was a nightmare. The boardwalk at Atlantic City was gone, like it never existed, and she hadn't been able to contact anyone from New York City. Someone from D.C. told her it wasn't too bad there but things were still shut up tight. No word about any government officials. From D.C. to Boston— no power, no media, only individuals on the radio trying to relay messages.

Monday August 22

After work I sat on the back deck watching the bees flying

around the flowering vines across our back fence where the tomato plants used to be. I must have dozed off. Dad startled me awake. I didn't know where he'd been.

"Check this out," he said and showed me *The South Florida Times:*

Paid Volunteers Would be Infected with O-meg For Vaccine Studies

How is this stupid paper even getting down here at this point? I handed it back to him and bent to take off my sneakers and sweaty socks. Even the humid air felt good moving through my toes.

"Well, we know it might not be such a big deal to be 'infected,'" I said and flung my socks across the porch in the direction of the washing machine.

"True, but where did they get the 'volunteers,' and what exactly will they be infected with?" He folded the paper. "I know, I know, I sound paranoid."

"No, you sound concerned." I stood up. "But do you think that type of news will really affect us down here?" Trying to focus on our lives here on the island was my new motivation.

"You're right," he said and hugged me. Holding on to him, I felt older, like I really was growing up.

Tuesday August 23

A new mark on the map—Tropical Storm Karl, low and quick, passed over Haiti this morning. I had to count on my fingers, Karl was number 11. We've had ELEVEN named storms so far.

At work, in the office Mike told me about Gil. The door was open and Pam stood five feet away at the first register slowly wiping down the area.

"He's going to Naples where my Mom lives. Apparently US I is still passable, if you have the right vehicle." He turned and looked at me. "It's not that Gil asked me to stay, but I know this store is everything to him. His dad started it. When I place meat orders or call in the payroll, I know I'm keeping something going, something my family built. We…I'm part of this community."

Pam's register beeped, the drawer slid open and she started to count change. Mike still looked at me. I listened, would not look away. "No one forced me into the family business. I spent summers here since I could walk. Uncle Gil would have me stock the bottom shelves."

From the office window, I saw bottles of shampoo on the bottom shelf were pushed around and out of place. I thought I would straighten them when I went back to my register, but he stepped out of the office and did it, getting down on one knee to turn them so the labels were facing out.

"Sometimes I feel like a country hick for choosing to come down here instead of finishing college, for not wanting to leave now." He turned to me. "I'm not ready to leave. Gil will take care of my mother. They'll be okay."

I just nodded. He wasn't leaving. I heard a "yet" in his voice. I didn't want to speak.

Thursday August 25

Make that Hurricane Karl. Usual prep under way. At the

store I heard all emergency services were being suspended, those that were left. Cops, firefighters, Coasties, any that were still around were evacuating. After Gaston no one outside of Old Town wanted to take any chances. We were really on our own, during and after, no matter what happened.

Friday August 26

Trip to the Grotto tonight. The hospital never reopened, but TJ kept an ambulance and a lot of people had his home number so he stayed home.

When we left the house I turned towards Mike's street. I hadn't seen him since he told me about Gil leaving. Pam's ground floor apartment flooded during Gaston, but she was still living there even with the damage and mold. When this new storm showed up Mike insisted she stay at the house. I bet it'll help distract from the fact that Gil left two days ago.

Pam stood on the porch smoking one of her long thin brown cigarettes. Her blonde hair was pulled back in a ponytail revealing an inch of dark brown roots mixed with gray.

"Well, I doubt you all are here to see me," she said and yelled for Mike. She lifted a red plastic cup dripping with condensation to my Dad. "Say hello to Mary for me."

"You bet," he replied as Mike came out on the porch.

Becky told me later that Mike's face "lit up" when he saw *ME*.

On the walk Mike mentioned he was usually back in Naples by this time of the year getting ready to go back to college. He also told me he hadn't heard anything from Gil or his mom.

We stopped for a single car to go through the intersection of Truman and Windsor—the light had just been blinking yellow since power came back after Gaston. At least it's still standing.

After lighting candles we stood around for a few minutes. Becky and Carol were talking quietly while Evie played with the dogs, Dad watched them all run and roll in the grass. In the relative calm and candlelight I reached for Mike's hand. We clasped fingers easily. He held tight and didn't let go until he went up the steps of Gil's house. Within the hour I imagined his windows and doors were shut as tight as ours against the coming storm.

Saturday August 27...Sunday August 28???

The days of storming blended together. I lost track of the hours. Probably should be used to it by now, but no.

Karl was a little late, and it didn't get bad until way after dark on Friday. Shortly after we got back to the house from the Grotto the weather radio announced Karl had strengthened to a Category 3 with winds of 115 mph. After the crazy flooding from Gaston Dad thought it would be better to be at TJ's with its extra two feet of elevation.

"Every little bit helps," he said as we trudged down Elizabeth Street in our rain coats and rubber boots. Evie ran ahead jumping in all the puddles. No lights were on at Gil's, or I guess it's Mike's now. Anyway, TJ's door was still open. Dad was the first one up the stairs.

"I was just coming to get you," TJ said as he appeared, filling the open doorway.

"Damnit, I must be slipping," Dad said as they hugged.

"I should have thought of the flooding, of the possibility of it strengthening."

"No worries, brother. We're all together now." Dad's knuckles were white as he clasped TJ's shoulder but he smiled as he turned to Becky and me, and told us to round up some board games.

Different location, same routine. Becky and I dug out the board and card games from a closet in the attic space that used to be Dad and TJ's shared bedroom. And then we waited. Dad shuffled cards over and over. But the board games remained closed. Carol sat upright in a chair, eyes closed, clutching empty knitting needles. Evie snuggled with the dogs, nestled between them on the floor under the big kitchen table. Becky sat at the table, her feet resting on Sargent's back. There was a crossword puzzle in front of her, and she held a pencil, but in the light of the Coleman lamp I saw the puzzle was empty. I sat at the table and thought about writing, but that's as far as I got. TJ sat by the front door.

We snacked on peanut butter crackers and small cans of V8, and napped when possible, moving from chair to couch to floor, wherever there was room. No games or nostalgic stories this time—we had nothing to add to the howling of Mother Nature.

Monday August 29

Today we awoke to the silence of an early morning breeze and easy rain that stopped by the time the sun came up. TJ opened the shutters and raised the windows to a street full of more branches and another carpet of green leaves, this time the small buds that had just begun to grow after Gaston. Thanks, Karl.

"How can there be this many branches left?" Becky asked.

No one answered, Evie reached up and took hold of her hand. A palm tree had fallen across the street and lay on top of a small house.

"With each storm more and more trees are exposed and vulnerable," TJ said. "Let's get started."

Becky and I took Evie and went to our house to begin clean up. Dad and the others stayed at TJ's. They started with the palm covering the road, silence broken by the revving chainsaw as we walked away. We didn't speak as we passed Mike's house. Pam stood in the open doorway in a long sleeveless sundress covered in swirls of color, smoking a cigarette. She gave us a thumbs up, then mimicked sleep and pointed behind her into the house as we passed. I looked away, the thought of Mike somewhere in the house maybe on a bed, eyes closed and relaxed in sleep, made my breath catch.

After about an hour of piling branches, raking and sweeping the front and back yard at home, I went upstairs to open windows and lay down. It was getting hot. Becky stayed out back sweeping and moving as much debris as possible into a large pile in the corner of the yard. She told me later she saw Evie squatting with her hands flat on the deck near the back door.

"I thought the pose a bit odd, but at the same time what is normal for Evie? When I heard the back screen door slam I figured she went in to get out of the sun." Becky paused and took a breath. "And then I heard it. I don't think I ever heard a real gunshot. But I knew what it was. I got to the front room seconds before you." She grabbed my hand.

We'd both arrived at the same time to see Evie with the gun. The gun that Dad had put on top of the book case, and it had been loaded with the bullets from the top of the refrigerator. A man lay face down on the floor just inside the house. He had a knife in one hand and an old pillowcase in the other, a pool of blood formed around his chest. Evie's arm was loose, hanging down by her side. She turned and looked at us, her eyes wet. I'd never seen her cry. As Becky walked towards her, Evie said "bad." Her voice was light, a whisper. She handed the gun to Becky then pushed her face into Becky's stomach. Instead of looking at the front door area, I looked at Becky and Evie, noticing how much Evie had grown. She must be three feet tall.

I didn't know how much time passed before I heard running from the street and my Dad burst onto the porch. He stopped when he saw the legs sticking out of the open front door.

"JJ," he said.

I looked into his clear blue eyes, then behind him I saw Mike. I moved my eyes to his. He looked scared.

"We're all okay," I said in a whisper.

I heard another voice behind them. "Who has the gun?"

"I do," Becky said.

"Okay, we're coming in." The voice sounded familiar.

A guy in a police t-shirt and jeans walked in ahead of Dad and Mike. Dad pushed past him and hugged me while the guy in the police tee took the gun from Becky. I kept my head on Dad's chest and closed my eyes, breathing in his warm scent. My eyes filled with tears, and my throat tightened painfully.

"Hey JJ," Dad said, rubbing his hand over the back of my head and down my neck, I remembered him lying on the couch with me on his chest comforting me the same way after my mom left. Right then I wanted to fall asleep standing up.

"Look who I ran into. Remember Scottie Watson?"

I opened my eyes.

"Hey Josie," he said with a brief smile before turning to examine the body. He kicked the knife away. Then I remembered him kicking a soccer ball with Becky and me in the middle of the street during the summer before we went into sixth grade. The Watsons lived on the next street over. He was in high school at that time and would come over in the afternoon to watch Becky and me if Dad was running late.

I smiled into Dad's chest and looked over at Becky. She sat at the table with Evie, who had her face buried in Becky's neck.

"I think Evie saved us," she said.

"I'd say you're right," Scott said. "I'm going to turn him over. Mike would you help with his legs."

"Sure," Mike said. When he passed me I felt his fingertips lightly brush the back of my hand that held onto my Dad.

"He used to only hit places at night," Scott said, when he could see the guy's face. "A couple of people got him on camera a few months ago before the storms got bad and the power outages messed with the security systems."

"I don't think I've seen him at the store," Mike said.

"Nothing's been reported lately so I wasn't sure he was still around. Of course not many people are left to report anything. I don't know what he would've done had he known you all were here."

I pulled away from Dad as more feet stomped outside, then TJ and Carol appeared on the front porch. Becky rose with Evie sill clutched to her chest.

Carol whispered, "Jesus."

"We're fine," Becky said. "We're all fine."

After that TJ and Scott loaded the guy up in TJ's pick-up, Dad left with them. No one asked where they were going. Becky and Evie went upstairs.

Mike looked down at the blood. "I'll go to the store and get bleach."

"I'll help," Carol said.

Mike put his hand on my shoulder. I wanted to hug him, I wanted him to hold me like my Dad had, to let me know it would be okay. Mike squeezed my shoulder.

"Go upstairs. Rest. When you come down again this will be done."

I went up and got in bed with Becky. She was already asleep, Evie curled into her. She turned and looked at me, her eyes completely hazel, no iris. I lay on the other side of her and she slid away from Becky just enough that her cool back molded into my chest. I slept immediately. Hours later when we came downstairs the back door was open, a breeze moving through the living room area, the smell of bleach lingering. A rug with a faded bird of paradise print that I didn't recognize covered the floor where the blood had been. Becky and Evie went to sit out back.

I stared at the rug until I heard Dad's whistle as he walked down the street. I couldn't face questions, concern, or worse ignoring what had happened, as if it had just been another day cleaning up from another hurricane. I went back upstairs to my own room.

———

Thunder decreases, the sun will return. Seeva leaves the notebook and walks out of the room wanting to find sun. The cooling rain, the violent entry. One needs warmth. The clouds move away, the sun has crossed over and shines onto the balcony. One imagines, at this time, a human would draw the thin covering over the door to block the sun. Seeva stands in the open doorway with closed eyes, absorbing.

Before returning to the room, Seeva looks at the jagged skyline of broken buildings, some leaning like a row of chipped teeth. Low buildings stand, hollow. All sit in a new ocean that started the year of Josie's journal.

Tuesday August 30

The house was empty and quiet all day. I sat on the back porch in the shade watching the ceiling fan circle in the breeze. Of course power had been out since Karl. I think the power will be out forever now. There were no more official services left on the island. Pepper stayed with me, sleeping under the table. Dad stopped in briefly to say he invited Scott for dinner. He sounded so normal. I wondered if that was hard for him to maintain.

Getting tired of myself, I snapped for Pepper and we headed to Mike's. He was on the street in front of his house.

"I was coming to invite you to dinner," I told him.

"I was coming to see how you were doing." He bent to rub Pepper's ears.

"Good," we both said.

He looked at me with raised eyebrows.

I shrugged. "I'm okay, I guess. It's not like I have anything to compare it to."

"I think you just described life as we know it now," he rubbed my shoulder and squeezed. I had to blink back tears. Dad had been out with TJ and Scott all day. Becky went over to see Carol before I even got out of bed. Inhaling, I told myself it was just from being alone too much today.

"Dinner would be nice." He smiled and ran his hand down my arm to grab my hand.

Dad made a vegetable soup on the gas grill, then let it cool, gazpacho like. It was too hot for hot food. The breeze had died at sunset. We sat on the back deck with the ceiling fan on low. Amazingly the solar panels survived the storm.

"I thought all emergency personal left?" I asked Scott. He sat across from Becky, Evie and me. Her skin is the color of cinnamon and she's about the size of a skinny toddler. But her hair hasn't grown, still a pixie length slightly lighter than her skin.

"Some stayed. But on their own, there aren't any more 'official' services being offered." He tipped back in the plastic chair then came forward laughing when it wobbled.

"Same with the hospital," TJ said. "I have a fully stocked ambulance at my house but the hospital was completely destroyed by Gaston. I haven't been over to see what's left above water now."

"Don't bother, there's nothing there," Scott said.

"How're your parents?" Dad asked.

"They left after Gaston. The flooding was too much even though it never reached their house. Dad has a brother in South Carolina." He picked up his bowl to drain the cold broth. "They planned on coming back after hurricane season but I haven't been able to get a hold of them. The land line at their house isn't working."

Becky and I started to pick up the empty bowls but Mike took them from us and gently nudged me back to my chair. Evie pulled a chair next to the sink. She held a dish towel—ready to dry.

"I haven't heard from my mother, and she's just in Naples," Mike said as he filled the sink with soap and water. The plumbing still worked but we only drank from the rain barrels after boiling the water.

"I've been trying to get someone from Naples on the radio. Want me to check on South Carolina for you, Scott?"

Over the sound of the running water, I didn't hear what town they were in. I watched out of the corner of my eye how easily Mike interacted with Evie. She seemed to put everyone at ease. At that point she was not even three months old, looked like a skinny child but had the calm disposition of an adult, like a very Zen adult.

"Are you staying in their house?" I zoned back into the conversation at the table.

"Yeah, I moved in after they left. I have a condo across from Smathers Beach but the first floor was flooded after Gaston. There hasn't been any power since then and after this storm I don't expect it to come back on anytime soon."

"I heard all the ground floor units were destroyed," Carol said. She'd taken out her knitting, this piece was orange. She'd been quiet during the meal. She'd been quiet lately.

"Yep, and I just talked to someone who is still living on the fourth floor. He said there's still about two feet of water covering the grounds. Apparently, people are using kayaks and paddle boards to get over to the dry parts of White Street."

"It's getting harder and harder," Dad said.

I turned to look at him. TJ was folding his napkin like a fan. Mike kept washing the dishes and handing them to Evie. Carol got up and went out on the front porch with Becky.

No one asked Dad to be more specific. I wondered if it might ever feel easy again.

Wednesday August 31

And now Lisa, a tropical storm then a hurricane then back to a tropical storm, all the while slowly battering the Bahamas, with the outer bands drenching us. At the store inventorying stock with Pam this morning she joked the island was going to sink.

It started to rain in the afternoon and got heavy by early evening. At least it cooled us off. Now, when it rained we ran outside in whatever we were wearing, or if there was time, we put on bathing suits for a shower courtesy of Mother Nature.

Thursday September 1

Lisa ravaged the Bahamas. The eye gathered strength as it moved into the Gulf and is now headed to Texas. Dad said someone on the radio made a reference to the book *Isaac's Storm*…I remember reading it for AP English Junior year—the island community of Galveston wiped away by a wall of storm water and debris from one of the deadliest, strongest hurricanes on record. Nice reference.

From the radio Dad also learned no colleges or universities in Florida, Louisiana or Georgia reopened for the fall semester. Many didn't even have summer session because of the O-meg crisis. The Governor was concerned about people coming and going in the three states with so much still unknown.

"Funny to think all the hype and panic over a virus, and it ends up hurricanes might just wipe us all out," Dad said with a smile as he kissed the top of my head and left the house. He didn't say where he was going.

I didn't reply. Calling for Pepper, I decided to go for a walk. The sun was setting, and the air had cooled a few degrees, taking the edge off the humidity. I'd spent the morning at the store with Mike. Becky and Evie were gone. To Carols? I didn't know. I didn't feel like chasing anyone down for company.

Pepper squatted at the base of a tree stump. I sat on the curb and watched a mama chicken scratch and peck in a pile of dirt on the sidewalk, showing her chicks how to find food.

Saturday September 3

No more business as usual. We have to create the usual from now on. Only Old Town is dry. It's been a week since Karl and then with the rain from Lisa who knows when, or if, the water will go down. And, who knows how many people are left—a few hundred, a couple thousand?. Dad, TJ and Scott went around the island by boat this morning with a loud speaker offering help and announcing Old Town as dry, safe.

Becky and I took the dogs and wandered around the neighborhood. Evie walked between the dogs. No one said much. It was like I didn't know what to say anymore. There were hardly any standing tress left so we went in the morning before the sun got too high. I knew Mike was at the store, he usually sets up outside and goes in with a flashlight if someone needs something. He and Pam had moved anything that was rotting out back and then moved anything non-perishable to the front of the store. And, he's not taking cash, it's all trade now.

Everything has shifted. Becky is with Evie, Dad is working with TJ constantly, and now Scott. I've lost track of Carol. So much has changed, I feel like I'm losing track of a lot.

Sunday September 4

I spent the morning hanging out in front of the store with Mike. We sat on milk crates in the shade. An old woman came by with a huge, fragrantly ripe mango. Mike gave her four cans of white beans for it.

"Kind of steep," I joked.

He winked at me. When the sun came around we put the milk crates in the store and locked up. He held the mango in both his hands, put it to his nose and inhaled.

"Smell," he held it out to me.

"I know what mango smells like," I said as I leaned forward.

"Now, imagine vanilla ice cream."

I pulled back. "That's mean."

He laughed, grabbed my hand and started to run towards his house.

"Nooo," I pulled back and started to walk, but held onto his hand. "Are you crazy—it's too hot to run!"

"I have a surprise—an emergency pint of vanilla ice cream on ice." He squeezed my hand. "A bit soupy, I imagine, but still cold enough. And now we have a mango."

I loved hearing him say "we."

We spent the afternoon in his shaded backyard, each with a big bowl of melted vanilla ice cream and thick chunks of mango. It tasted like cool sunshine. It tasted normal.

Happy Labor Day, if that still means anything. It used to mean no school. It used to mean a holiday weekend full of tourists. Even being a Monday doesn't have any significance at this point. If it weren't for this journal and a humidity warped ASPCA 2016 calendar on the fridge I wouldn't know the day of the week, let alone the date. Does it even matter anymore?

Thursday September 8

Cloudy few days meant minimal solar charge which meant no fan last night, and no breeze either. When the sun came up this morning on a clear sky Dad declared the solar panels were happy. I hadn't slept much so I stayed in the house, out of the sun, all day. I didn't know where Becky was, although I knew she'd be somewhere with Evie and maybe Carol. Sargent and Pepper were both gone, not surprising, Sargent was pretty attached to Evie. Dad had left a note. He and TJ were out trying to get an idea of anyone else left in the Mid and New Town areas, and see what was still flooded.

Feeling a little stir crazy by late afternoon, I went over to Mike's and ended up helping Pam feed a bunch of stray cats. She said Mike was upstairs reading or maybe sleeping. I blushed at the idea of him in his bedroom. Seeing my face, Pam laughed herself into a coughing fit, then motioned for me to come along with her.

"They can take care of themselves," she said, pointing to a small black and white cat stalking a lizard. "But I'll keep putting food out as long as we have it." She shook the bag at the corner and four cats came running. We gave them each a small pile of food.

We walked in silence. Pam walked slow, it was nice to be

outside, even in the late afternoon sun. We laughed about crossing the street looking for shade.

The sunny side of the street is no longer a positive phrase.

Saturday September 10

According to Dad and TJ, Mid and New Town were completely flooded. There were still some people staying in stilt houses or second floors and there were some living in the high school, taking over classrooms.

Tuesday September 13

Stormy, rainy and windy yesterday and today. The streets were clogged with puddles and leaves again. We went out at sunset to try to sweep some of it away so the water might drain. Supposedly all that weather was nothing tropical.

It was nice to have a break from the sun. Still no electricity so the cloudy skies and wind were welcome. Actually, I don't know why I wrote "still." There will be no more electricity, at least in the regular modern way. What we have now is from solar, and it's just enough for some lights and fans. Welcome to the new twenty-first century, Key West.

Wednesday September 14

Okay, I was wrong—that was Tropical Storm Matthew. We had the weather radio off for a couple of days. After raining and blowing over us, it strengthened, then really hit Central Florida, barreling across the middle of the state starting at Punta Gorda and traveling up through Orlando. I think Mickey's been displaced. Having never been to Disney World, I didn't even know what that might mean, other than a lot of people in Florida out of work and probably heading for drier ground. If there even is a tourist industry left? Or any industry left in Florida?

I was just coming out of my room when I heard Mike downstairs. He'd come over to use our phone.

"I'm still trying to call my mom," I heard him say. "I can't get through on the land line at the house. I just want to make sure it's not a problem with my line."

"You don't have to explain anything, son," Dad assured him.

I stopped and stood at the top of the stairs when I heard Dad say that word. He'd never had a reason to call anyone "son."

It was only about a minute before I heard the clack of the phone being put back into the cradle on the wall. I didn't think I'd made any noise but he looked up the stairs and gave me a little wave, with a shake of his head. I wanted to have him stay with us. I wanted him to feel safe here. I wanted this to be his home but knew that wasn't possible as long as he worried about his own family.

Thursday September 15

Aaand, look—one right after another rolling through the Atlantic toward the Lesser Antilles—Nicole and Otto. Nicole just barely a tropical storm, probably sucked into Otto soon. Otto is already a hurricane—big and fast. More marks on the tracking map, and the weather radio is back on.

Becky and I talked today. It feels like forever since we really talked. We were out back getting water from one of the rain barrels and saw smoke coming from the direction of Stock Island. We both turned at the same time and sniffed. Then Evie came out of the house and pointed to the north.

"Fire," she said. "But, okay." She speaks little, as in uses as few words as necessary to be understood.

"Stay here and wait for Robbie," Becky told her. "Josie and I will go to the top of Garrison Bight Bridge and try to see something."

We walked to the end of Fleming Street to the small convenience store that now stood in a foot of water, windows boarded, glass door broken. Becky and I had waded in with flashlights a month ago, the shelves were empty. It was the kind of place that mainly carried beer and various brands of chips. I imagined it'd been cleaned out early.

There were a bunch of kayaks on a dry section of the parking lot, tied to a pile of concrete blocks. The water rose and lowered with the tides. Dad and TJ had found them around the Bight from one of the abandoned kayak tour companies. We didn't lock them or anything, there were always a few there to use.

We untied two and dragged then into the water. Pushing off in the shin deep water, we paddled silently down the murky waterway of what used to be Palm Drive. Still getting used to the new silence, I noticed how things had been reshaped. The hedge around the military housing was gone. The houses had not been built to withstand tropical storms, let alone hurricanes—so a few were heaps of splintered wood and others were missing roofs. On the other side sat the low income housing, cheap looking cinder block structures that still stood. A couple of kids waved to us from a second story window. They smiled, I imagine still thinking this was some kind of fun adventure—way better than school. Hadn't I thought something similar a couple of months ago?

"I think it's coming from Mount Trashmore," I said as we pulled the kayaks up to the dry inclined pavement and walked the remaining fifteen feet to the top of the bridge. There was a thin stream of smoke in the distance. The remnants of Hilton Haven, another line of flooded and shredded houses, blocked our view of the old dump facility.

"That's not a lot of smoke and Evie said it's okay." Becky put her hand up to the end of her visor.

"So, Evie knows things?" I asked as we walked back down the bridge. The early afternoon sun was high and strong. I tried to not leave the house at this time of day anymore.

"Yes, she does. Remember the shooting?"

My stomach dropped, I felt queasy but tried to make a joke. "Gee, no, Becky, remind me again?"

She elbowed me. "Ha-ha, funny, J. Anyway, she knew that guy was no good." We reached the kayaks, she was pulling hers into the water. "She likes Mike," she added. "Why do you think your Dad is okay with you being over there, like all the time?"

I dropped the end of my kayak. Even through the weave of my straw hat the top of my head felt hot. "I am not always over there! No more than you're over at Carol's with Evie, or out scouting the island with my Dad." I almost said something about having no one of my own. But that would make it seem like I was using Mike, as a default. And, that wasn't it. The skin on my shoulder was stinging. I could feel it burning, I had to get out of the sun soon.

"I like Mike, I really do," I said quietly, bending to pick up the end of my kayak again. "But, I miss you."

Becky looked sad, I imagine she squinted behind her sunglasses. Her kayak was floating, she stood ankle deep in the water.

"I know, Josie. It's all so different. I'm also getting to know Evie, what she is, what I am now. What it means. And I guess now I know how you must have felt, to be left out, ignored, like I did with each new boyfriend I rolled through." She pulled at the brim of her visor, bringing it lower. "I miss you, too. I'm trying to not be jealous of Mike, or of what you two have."

I didn't know what we had, I thought, bending to push my kayak into the water. I held the end of the line, the so-called bitter end. "That all seems like so long ago. It feels like we were so young, compared to what's going on now."

"Now?" Her kayak floated out and bumped into mine.

I motioned around us. Sailboats were piled against the bridge, rigging and anchor lines tangled, metal snapped, masts toppled. We were about fifteen feet up the bridge, surrounded by the sea where there used to be docks and a parking lot.

"I don't know. You're a mother, and I think I'm in love." My throat burned. I really felt like crying

Becky waded over, still holding the line for her kayak and hugged me. My throat closed. I clutched her, and held on, even though we were both sweating.

"I'm glad Josie, really. I think those are both very good things for us."

"Crap, we've grown up, haven't we?" I asked.

She pulled back smiling. "Did we have a choice?"

I still didn't know what it meant, but I felt better—safe with Becky.

Sunday September 18

Dad and TJ went to Mount Trashmore this morning. They'd untangled some of the boats in the Bight, and maneuvered slowly through the sea plane basin. Evie went with them, swimming ahead of them out of the harbor looking for anything under the water that might cause any problems—sunken boats, missing channel markers. Dad also wanted her along to get a sense if any of the people might be a little…off.

"We don't need any negative energy in the neighborhood." I didn't ask what he would have done if Evie questioned anyone. Or what he would have done if any of them questioned Evie. After four trips they brought back almost twenty people. They'd been camping there for the last month since Karl. It was a mix of people, young and old, Key Westers looking more bedraggled and sweaty than usual. Cutoff jeans, ripped t-shirts, faded sundresses, torn fishing shirts over darkly tanned skin.

While they were gone, Mike had scoped out some of the big empty houses in the neighborhood. Becky and I went through looking for anything that might be of value or returned for at some point. We left lists and notes of what we took tucked into drawers. Mike stored things like photo albums, yearbooks and framed photos in one of the walk-in coolers at Gil's. It was nice, the three of us doing something together. With so few of us left here, everyone had to work together.

Monday September 19

As Otto approached more people left. Even the majority of the people that just came from Stock Island headed out. TJ said the Fort Meyers Ferry was going to run trips on Wednesday. The ferry that used to bring tourists from the West coast hadn't made a trip down here in a while. But Gaston and then Karl, it was too much for some. With the airport closed and rumors about US 1...Mike also heard all the government officials, even the city mayor, went up to Key Largo before Karl. They were giving up on us, giving up on all the Keys.

Walking around, I wondered if this area would still be dry in a couple of decades. It was the highest point of the island, but at 18 feet above sea level that wasn't much comfort.

Wednesday September 21

Last ferry left tonight. Carol was on it. Becky didn't seem surprised. I checked on her before going to bed. We are on "farmer's hours" as Dad calls it—to bed and rise with the sun.

"Carol's been pulling away for a few weeks, since the shooting. Apparently she's been thinking about going up to my mom's place," Becky told me.

We were in her room, Evie sat on the floor working a 1000 piece puzzle.

"Has she even heard from your mom?"

"They've been talking on the phone. I guess the one at the propane office still worked. I think she got a little freaked out by everything. My mom is staying in some big government run complex. They took over a row of hotels in Orlando. Moved there after

Matthew. Carol wanted me to go with her." Becky sat on the floor next to Evie. I wondered if her mom had asked for her. Becky shook her head. "That wasn't going to happen, for many reasons."

Sitting by her on the floor, I picked up a border piece and put it in place.

"I'm sorry, Becky."

Evie pointed to a puzzle piece by Becky's foot. She picked it up and connected it to mine. "Don't be. I'm with my family."

Carol was gone. Mike was still here. I felt guilty, and nervous.

Thursday September 22

Boarded up and waiting for Otto.

After Carol's departure, I had trouble sleeping. I couldn't help but wonder if Mike had left too. His own mother was supposedly still in Naples. What reason did he have to stay here? I knew what I wanted the answer to be. Anyway, I started for his place soon after I had a cup of tea this morning. I didn't make it far, he was coming up the steps to our front porch.

"Hey," he said.

I smiled with relief. "Hey."

I could not stop smiling at the sight of him, rumpled hair, lighter than it'd been when I first met him. Inside my brain was screaming, *there is a Category 4 hurricane heading right for this tiny speck of an island that you call home, what are you smiling about?*

He's still here, he's still here, were the other words in my head.

"We're getting ready to start the domino games. We're playing for cigarettes," he said with a laugh. I was still smiling. Like a fool. I laughed.

You're still here. You are still here.

"Pam's stash of cigarettes versus what I still have at the store," he said. He was wearing a faded blue Gil's Groceries t-shirt with the sleeves cut off.

I swallowed. "Those are high stakes," I told him. I wanted to invite him in, have him stay here with me, with my family.

"I should be okay. I won't allow her to smoke in the house but she can drink as much as she wants."

"Is that fair?" I wanted to hug him. I wanted to hold onto him.

"According to my uncle, everything is fair game when playing dominos with a Conch." At the mention of Gil his brow wrinkled.

"Okay, well, have a nice hurricane," I said with a grin and thumbs up. I think my hand shook.

He laughed. "You too, Josie." He grabbed my hand, gave it a squeeze, then turned away from me, and walked back down the stairs. It was still sunny at that point, but I felt the wind changing. That was hours ago and it was still quiet.

We were hunkered down at TJ's, seeking the solace of that extra few feet of elevation. We boarded up tight for this one, pieces of plywood even over the closed shutters. The latest report had Otto at a Category 4 and still strengthening. Dad and TJ took down the solar panels yesterday as an added precaution.

I guess this was the calm before the storm. No consistent wind yet, but it felt like the pressure dropped. We marked the latest spot on our chart, as of about an hour ago the leading edge was close.

Friday September 23

Otto turned at the last moment—crashed into Homestead and Miami as a Category 5. We got nothing, literally nothing—no wind above maybe 25 mph, no rain. I swear if we'd left plastic chairs on the front porch they'd still be there. As soon as we heard the forecast and new coordinates taking Otto away from us Dad and I opened the shutters to let in the early morning light and fresh air as the others slept. We sat on TJ's front porch listening to birds, watching the sky brighten. I've missed spending time with him, but didn't want to ruin the silence and calm with any heavy talk. We were safe, all of us, that's what I knew, that's all I needed to know right then.

Saturday September 24

Maybe things were getting too intense for some people, the few people left. Someone broke into Gil's last night and stole four cases of soup. One of the glass doors was broken. It ended up being so calm while everyone waited for the storm. The break in could have happened at any time.

It hasn't exactly been a lucky hurricane season this year, but we got very very lucky with Otto. Not so the rest of South Florida. Dad had been trying to reach some of his regular contacts throughout the area. Nothing. Even the phone land lines were dead.

Sunday September 25

Soup theft solved.

I was hanging with Mike in front of the store—how I

spend my mornings now. Scott walked down the sidewalk behind two guys about my age. They each carried two boxes of soup. Mike and I sat on our milk crates on the sidewalk. I recognized the guys from school. They lived in the neighborhood in a huge restored ship captain's house. The taller one had a bandanna on to keep his overgrown hair out of his eyes. He would have been a senior this year, his brother, two years younger, just completed ninth grade. They both ran with the cross country team.

After sheepishly apologizing while Scott stood back, the younger one in ragged cut offs spoke.

"It's just so freaky around here," he said. "I mean, who's left? Where is everyone?" His voice rose. "And why are we still here? Why haven't our parents sent for us?"

"We don't know what to do," his taller brother said. Both were severely tanned. "Our parents sent us down here last year to live with our grandparents. But they are so old. I think they'd be happy to just die here. It feels like we're just sitting around waiting for the world to end or something." He rubbed his hands on the torn thighs of his jeans.

Mike nodded at Scott. "I'll forget the soup and broken window. But I need help cleaning out and organizing the store. Come by tomorrow morning. When the job is done you can each take a case of soup." He held his hand out to the older brother.

"Okay, okay," he nodded. "I'm Sam. That's Jeff. Thank you." He shook Mike's hand then tapped the other boy on the shoulder.

Jeff looked in Mike's direction, but his eyes weren't focusing. He seemed to be looking over Mike's shoulder, at nothing. "Okay, yeah, thanks." Then he followed Sam down the street.

"I've seen them running all over town," Scott said, wiping his forehead with the bottom of his t-shirt. "But I haven't seen the grandparents since I moved back in the neighborhood. I'm afraid they're holed up in that house waiting for the rapture."

"I'll keep the boys busy for a few days," Mike said.

Watching them walk down the street, I wanted to run home and hug my Dad. Instead without thinking, I grabbed Mike's hand. It was warm and a little damp.

"The young one looked so scared." Mike squeezed my hand. "He's not that much younger than you, Josie."

I felt older, so much older. I needed to make a joke.

"About the same difference in age as us," and I squeezed back, not believing I used the word "us." He didn't reply, but he also didn't release my hand. I don't remember when we broke the hold.

Monday September 26

Mike and TJ raided the big supermarkets out on the boulevard. It was under like five feet of water even at low tide. They took a flats boat as close as they could up to the bridge before the Overseas Market and then close to the sea wall across from Searstown. From each point they kayaked in. The old Publix was the best, since it was up almost ten feet above the parking lot. They didn't even bother with the new Publix, the water was almost to the top of the doors. Winn Dixie wasn't as bad but the only things they could scavenge were on the top shelves.

He told me about it as we walked to Ft. Zach. As the only natural beach on the island Ft. Zach was still there. The water was higher, the pines were gone or stripped, and the current was really strong, so we only waded. Looking out at the horizon, it still felt normal there. It still felt like Key West, like a cruise ship or sailboat could appear on the horizon.

Tuesday September 27

Dad's been on the radio all morning. He couldn't reach anyone. No reports from the mainland, even Key Largo.

Wednesday September 28

Dad finally found a radio broadcast this morning: a doctor warning people to stay out of South Florida or leave the state altogether. Facilities damaged, power lines down, no electricity, water quality questionable, medical supplies running out. That morning he'd treated a case of what he suspected was cholera.

Thursday September 29

Thinking about yesterday's radio broadcast, with every storm we had become more and more isolated. This time it felt complete. TJ heard the 18 mile stretch was barely passable, a lot of US 1 is washed over with almost a foot of sand, and the bridge on Card Sound road was gone.

I kept picturing the younger brother, Jeff, who stole the soup, his glazed eyes, his raised voice. His fear.

Seeva remembers that fear, feeling it in the humans, seeing it on faces, hearing it in voices. They did not know what to do with O-megs. They did not understand, so they tested, and contained, thought they could control. Before Cloyal came, it was everywhere, that fear. Then the humans left, unlocked the doors and Seeva waited, focusing on Cloyal. While Seeva waited, humans continued to leave; some stayed, some were left behind. Any who carried O-meg were taken.

When Cloyal brought Seeva out of the hills towards the water, they went to the Municipality where Cloyal said they would be safe and welcome. On their way, around the cities the fear was still heavy. Seeva felt it, Cloyal pushed them on knowing there could be no rescue, no help when it was that strong. Once they passed those areas, Seeva would breathe in the air, fresh with trees, sometimes smoke and then the smell of the sea.

Seeva inhales, there is no fear here.

Monday October 3

Weather radio still works—there's another storm, Paula, "only" a tropical storm, heading for South Florida.

We made a sweep of the island today, early morning. TJ and Dad stood on paddle boards, Becky and I each in two person kayaks and Evie swam. Mike stayed behind to check more houses in the neighborhood for any food or other supplies that might be used. We were under no illusion that the owners would be coming back.

Dad and TJ went up and down side streets. Becky and I kayaked slowly down what used to be White Street.

"I guess we should start calling this the White Street Canal?" Becky said.

There were very few trees left standing, and most palm trees had no fronds left. Just rows of large toothpick looking things. They'll fall soon enough from sitting in the sea water. Along the way we talked loudly, and yelled back and forth with Dad and TJ to let people, if there were any, know we were there and not a threat. Evie swam ahead, pausing, looking up at some spots, and waiting. There must still be people on the higher floors of the condos and hotels along Atlantic and South Roosevelt Boulevard. No one ever came out, but we saw kayaks, paddle boards and small boats tied up to railings at the water's surface.

It was breezy on the east side of the island, just enough to cool us off. We headed all the way around, past the East Martello fort and the airport.

"So strange," I said quietly. Becky stopped paddling and drifted back to me. Evie was in the kayak with her.

"You'll have to be more specific, Josie."

"Look to the left." We were just passing the entrance to the airport, the ramp up to the departure area was five feet deep in ocean water. There was a high tide line of sea weed two feet higher. I pointed up ahead to the restaurants with boarded up windows, water up past the bottom edge of the plywood, a couple of cars pushed up against the building, only the roofs visible. A tangle of downed power lines and a pile of branches and seaweed were pushed by low waves into the broken front door of one building.

"Total destruction. Even if the water recedes how long would it take to put it all back together, IF anyone even wanted to try?" I motioned to the right. "Then look over here."

The sea wall and large rocks that used to form a break water might still be there, but they were well under the ocean's surface. The sky was light blue, with a few clouds. Waves came in low ripples pushed by a light wind, the surface varying shades of blue to turquoise to brown indicating fluctuating depths and layers of seagrass. It looked like a postcard tourists used to buy indicating they had been to paradise—*wish you were here.*

Evie was stretched out in the front seat of Becky's kayak. She wasn't growing as quickly as she did the first few months. She wore a yellow one piece bathing suit and at almost four feet tall looked like a young girl. She did not wear sunglasses.

"Mother Nature won," she said.

We paddled the rest of the way around the island's new edge, ending where we started hours earlier, in the parking lot of the convenience store at the end of our street. Pulling the kayaks and paddle boards up on the wet pavement, we tied them to the concrete blocks, and walked home. No one had said anything since Evie's observation.

Tuesday October 4

Looks like Paula would be going just under us, although she was forecast to strengthen over the Gulf and hit the Panhandle with a vengeance.

Thursday October 6

Paula turned north earlier than expected and hit us as a Category 1 yesterday. The winds weren't so bad—kind of used to them now, just unexpected. And it rained, all last night and most of today. We went out this evening for a walk to check out damage, etc. First stop—Mike's. No one asked, just turned at the corner. The others stopped to help an old woman move a toppled palm that blocked her gate.

Mike and Pam sat on the front porch, Pam with one of her long thin cigarettes clutched between the fingers of her right hand.

"No time to prepare for that storm," he said. He wore a light blue tank top and navy basketball shorts. Happiness at the sight of him made my cheeks turn pink. I could feel it. I moved to the thin shadow of a tree trunk.

Pam exhaled smoke. Mike sighed loudly and waved his hand near his face.

"Why don't you just go for a walk with your little girl-friend," she said with a smile. I really felt my face heat up.

"It's too late for me to fire you, isn't it?" he asked as he stood up.

"If Gil never did, why would you? Plus I'd have to actually be working for money in order to be fired, right?" She took a drink from a red solo cup. Dad, Becky and Evie walked up.

"It's five o'clock somewhere," Dad said with a wave. She raised her cup to him and tried to laugh, but ended up in a long cough. Mike looked back at her as we walked away. She waved him on. As we walked around puddles, I asked if he'd heard anything from his mom.

"My land line stopped working a while ago," he said and went up to talk to Dad. Evie walked next to me.

No new damage. Everything that could be knocked down had been knocked down by now. A few small branches and more green leaves blew through the streets. A single shutter missing almost all the slates lay in the middle of the intersection of Southard and William. I glanced at the house where Sam and Jeff lived. It was shuttered, so I couldn't tell if anyone was inside or not.

Evie grabbed my hand and I looked away. I watched Mike a few feet ahead talking with Dad and TJ. Becky walked behind them. She turned and smiled at me but she looked sad. Evie gave my fingers a light squeeze.

Friday October 7

I sat with Dad last night listening to the radio. Things were bad. Paula just kept going and going, raking its way up the West coast of Florida, and across the panhandle. It then destroyed the coast of Louisiana and parts of Mississippi. The levies in New Orleans couldn't hold against the rain and storm surge. It was gone, under water. It was like the sea was staking a claim, or reclaiming its rightful place.

According to a woman Dad found from Gainesville there was no more Florida, Louisiana, or Georgia. What was left of those states and from the Panhandle down to just south of Orlando was called New Florida and Governor Suarez was in charge, governing from the mountains of what used to be Georgia. There was a quarantine on the southern part of the state from Clearwater, Tampa and St. Pete across to Melbourne. He ordered check points with an ID check and blood test for anyone trying to head north.

"I'd say we're cut off," Dad said. He put his arm around me and rubbed my back. "Between the O-meg panic and hurricanes across the country, no one will be coming down here to check on us."

I tried to read his voice, hear any fear of maybe triumph?

It was just us sitting in his radio room. It felt like a long time since it'd been just us.

"I think I feel safer," I said. "Better for Evie. And we'll be okay, right?" I stopped myself from calling him Daddy.

He leaned over, kissed the side of my head and inhaled. "We're going to be just fine, JJ."

We listened to the static for a few minutes, I wasn't ready to leave the room right away.

Saturday October 8

More news from the radio. Broadcasts being repeated on different stations.

"All hospitals are closed due to cumulative storm damage, lack of electricity, lack of sterile equipment and work areas."

"Boil water alert continues. Watch for symptoms of dengue, Ebola and cholera."

"Move to higher ground wherever possible."

"Leaving the state is recommended course of action for all remaining residents."

"State of South Florida is quarantined. Governor Suarez of New Florida reminds all residents to stay put until further notice."

Dad turned it off after the last two. We didn't stay in the radio room after that. Becky was just getting back with Evie and the dogs. Evie had caught a nice sized yellow tail snapper, almost half the size of her. Dad fired up the grill while Becky filleted and I headed to Mike's. I knew he had a bunch of coconuts in his backyard. I needed it to feel like a normal evening, or what passed for normal now, down here at the end of the road.

The sun is low, the sky's blue darkens. Reading about the radio broadcasts and news from the Dad, Seeva wonders if that was when the humans left, unlocked the door between them and Seeva, and walked away. Much changed after that storm. Cloyal says that was when the humans knew they were no longer in control and retreated.

Night air blows chilly through the empty window frame and open door. Seeva shivers. It is almost over.

Monday October 10

This morning Dad and I were at the table writing the contents on the lids of canned food with torn labels when a guy came up to the open door. It was still hot enough to keep doors and windows open for any breeze during the day. I heard the light knock on the door frame.

"Hello," the guy said with a slight Haitian accent. "My name is Louis." He wore cutoff jeans and a short-sleeved fishing shirt.

"We've seen you around the neighborhood and I decided to come here. I have some questions about …the girl."

I knew he wasn't talking about me. Dad stood and motioned for him to sit down.

He told us he'd gone home to Haiti in April and now worried he contracted O-meg.

"My girlfriend, Veronique, is pregnant."

"Why are you worried?" Dad asked. He leaned against the kitchen counter.

"I am one of nine siblings. This is not a normal pregnancy." Louis looked at me then Dad. His eyes were a deep blue.

Becky came in from the back porch with Evie. She'd been hanging laundry out to dry, her blonde hair, even brighter now from the sun, perched on top of her head in a bun. Evie, now about four feet tall, stopped and looked at Louis.

"How far along is she," Becky asked.

"Almost seven months." Louis was looking at Evie.

"Can we meet her?" Becky asked placing her hand on Evie's shoulder indicating they were a team, if one went the other went too.

"Please," Louis said as he stood. "We are staying on the second floor of the big brick building on the corner by the grocery store."

As Louis turned to leave Evie said, "Don't worry, she's okay." He turned and smiled at her.

Later, Becky found me at Mike's. We were sitting on the front porch steps discussing Pam. She hadn't been feeling well. Or as Mike said, she felt as well as she could feel with all her smoking and drinking.

"How are they?" I asked as she sat down.

"Freaked out," she said. "We compared notes and it's definitely an O-meg, which means she'll give birth any day. Evie stayed with her."

From inside the house Pam started coughing. When she

didn't stop after almost a minute Mike went in to check on her.

"I'll see you at home?" Becky asked.

I wrapped my hands around my knees and lay my head on my knees.

"Later," I said.

She ran her hands through the bangs that had fallen over my eyes. "Time for a cut, Auntie J."

As she walked away, I smiled to myself. A new nickname. I stayed on the porch listening to Mike's quiet voice through the open window. A skinny grey tabby cat crossed the street, a dead baby iguana hanging from his mouth.

We are better off down here, I told myself, away from everyone else, a fresh start.

Thursday October 13

The weather was changing. It felt like fall, just a bit. About an hour before sundown and the air felt drier, just a bit less humid, just a bit cooler, fresher, like summer and hurricane season might be coming to an end.

Friday October 14

Veronique gave birth this morning, an O-meg. Becky and Evie were there. The new one's name is Amber, a girl.

––––––––

Tonight a full moon will rise out of the broken horizon and sea that has invaded, claiming its new home. A damp breeze continues to blow in the room. Seeva puts down the notebook.

More. There are more.

Yes, comes from Cloyal.

Seeva exhales. Cloyal is returning, a full white moon lighting the way.

More.

Monday October 17

Another tropical storm, Richard, made it all the way to the coast of Newfoundland, too far out to sea for anyone to worry about. But still there, in waters that should be too cold by this time. And down here thousands of miles away, a cold front blew in last night. More wind, more rain but this time cold, or cold enough to shut windows and doors.

Tuesday October 18

Everyone has scattered again. Becky and Evie were with Amber's new family a lot. Dad, Scott and TJ took off most mornings, making the rounds by foot, bicycle, kayak or boat. They estimate there are a few hundred people left. Even Sargent and Pepper had separated—Sargent with Evie and Pepper with Dad. She was always more his dog anyway, so now he could take her everywhere with him.

I would help if asked, or knew of something I could do.

I stay close to Mike and Pam. He spends about an hour at the store in the mornings and another in the evenings, sitting on the milk crate outside in case anyone needed anything. There was still a good stash of non-perishable food inside. I stayed with

Pam, who was maintaining simply by keeping her wine intake at a certain level. She started to limit her cigarettes. Depending on the time of day and intensity of the sun, we sit on the front porch or in the backyard and read.

Mike pried the shutters open and broke a window to get into the library last week. It smelled pretty musty, like old books, really warm, old books, but at least it stayed dry. I went in and got novels to read, started with the A's. Sometimes Pam asked me to read aloud so she could "rest her eyes." It made me feel useful, even when she fell asleep. Mike told me she coughs through the night, so I thought this might be the only sleep she got.

Friday October 21

Life goes on. I don't know what to write about anymore. It stayed cool after the cold front. The humidity was down so the nights were comfortable. During the day the breeze didn't feel so much like hot air. Tonight would have been Goombay in Bahama Village, the kick off for Fantasy Fest. It was marked on the calendar stuck on the fridge.

Mike was over helping me wash the dogs with lemon juice. We'd been pouring lemon juice over ourselves all summer to help keep the mosquitos away, for the dogs it helped with fleas. Dad napped on the couch. Next door Evie played with Amber in the mossy green pool while Becky, Veronique and Louis chatted. As long as Sargent heard Becky's voice he was okay.

"You never went to any part of Fantasy Fest?" I asked. He'd been quiet lately. I was actually surprised he showed up this afternoon. He'd stayed at the store almost all day yesterday.

"Nope, I only stayed with Gil for the summer, then I'd head back north the middle of August." He dipped a large sponge in a bucket of water and squeezed it over Sargent's back.

"The actual Fantasy Fest parade was too crazy for me—way too many people, drunk or not—just too many. Goombay wasn't so bad, early enough that there weren't a lot of tourists-they waited for the wilder events later on like TuTu Tuesday, the Toga Party at Sloppy Joe's, Pretenders in Paradise." I had to grip Pepper's collar and squeeze the sponge over her, her tail tucked between her legs.

"I'd go with Becky unless it was a 'boyfriend year,' then I'd go with Dad and TJ. Usual street vendors sold twenty dollar plates of food you then had to sit on the curb to eat with a plastic fork."

Mike laughed and dumped a glass of water over Sargent who shook. Water filled the air. "You sure make this Goombay thing sound appealing."

"No it was. Good music and we always saw so many people we knew. Dad and TJ would see old friends from high school, or people who knew my grandparents. Everyone yelled *Hey Bubba, Look at you Cuzzie,* or *Brotha how's it goin'.* All night long, slaps on the back, big handshakes." I smiled remembering all the large voices, heavy hugs, and smiles.

"I wish you could have gone with us," I said.

He flicked water at me.

"Me too," he said, handing me the bottle of lemon juice to pour over Pepper's back after he'd done the same for Sargent. We worked the liquid into their fur and skin. Voices and quiet laughs came from next door. I thought of past Goombays, an event I never thought of missing, wondering where all the Bubbas, Brothas and Cuzzies were now.

I ran into Jeff and Sam on my way to Mike's this morning. Sam ran up to me.

"Hey, I think I convinced my grandparents we have to leave." His hair was longer with the back hanging past his shoulders. Jeff came up behind him, looking around but not at me or Sam. He wore a New England Patriots baseball cap.

"How," I asked. "Major portions of US1 washed away, a couple of the smaller bridges are gone."

"We're on our way to talk to Mike," he said. Jeff walked five paces behind looking over his shoulder every few feet. Sam continued. "The grandparents are finally waking up and now they're freaked out. Plus, it's all starting to get to Jeff. I really want to get out of here. It can't be any stranger on the mainland, can it?"

"Why talk to Mike?" I pushed, not wanting to consider his last question.

"He can sail. He told us about sailing down here over the summers when he was the same age as us. And I know he's worried about his mom. That's how it seemed anyway. So I was thinking if we could find a good enough boat maybe we could sail out of here."

I stopped, I couldn't catch my breath. We were on the corner but I couldn't turn down Mike's street. I left them and continued towards Duval Street. Sam called after me, "Um, have a nice day."

I spent the rest of the morning walking around what used to be the busiest, most congested street on the island—tourists walking in the streets, crowding the sidewalks, on bicycles or scooters, rental cars turning the wrong way down Fleming and Southard streets, pedi-cabs, food and beer delivery trucks—all hours, all days. Now, every shop, bar and restaurant was boarded up and broken in some way. I imagined rats and raccoons were the customers now. Fallen trees and tangled power lines covered the sidewalks where it looked like someone had tried to clear a path. Maybe in the hope of tourists returning? The smell of rotting leaves and food blew with the breeze.

I could only walk east as far as United before hitting water. I walked over to Whitehead and looked at what used to be the water's edge. The Southernmost Point stood in two feet of water sandblasted down to the concrete surface, with only small patches of red or black paint left. The rising sun warmed the dried sea weed and muddy sand. The smell drove me away as much as the standing water.

Turning, I walked in the other direction as far as Caroline Street. There were still enough buildings in the remaining three blocks before Mallory Square to block the horizon. It didn't matter, no one was left to applaud the setting sun. Everything was empty and quiet.

I almost missed the sounds of cars, scooters and tourists. I didn't want to think about the conversation taking place between Sam and Mike. I knew what was going to happen. I walked home fast, and played solitaire in my room until it was too dark to see the cards.

Monday October 24

I talked to Becky this afternoon as we washed towels on the back porch. I hadn't been to see Mike since I ran into Sam two days ago. I didn't want to hear what he might have to tell me.

"Mike's really worried about his mom," I blurted as soon as I dunked a large beach towel into the sun warmed water.

"I know," she said, grabbing a couple of small dish towels from the pile. "Your Dad's been trying to get a hold of someone from Naples on the radio. But there's nothing. He can't get anyone from anywhere in South Florida." She only dunked and squeezed the dish towels twice in the rinse bucket.

Not wanting to cry, I kept my eyes on clouds forming in the west. Rain would be nice to help rinse the towels on the line and refill buckets. A minute passed, I couldn't speak, just kept my hands submerged in the warm, soapy water, squeezing the towel until my fingers hurt. Sitting back on my heels, my soapy hands flopped on my thighs soaking my shorts, the water marks hid the stains.

"Josie?" Becky kept dunking and hanging dish towels.

I shook my head and tried to inhale, I wheezed.

She turned to look at me.

"Josie, will you go with him?"

I coughed out a sob and shook my head. My throat burned.

"No," I rasped. That much I knew.

Becky dropped a towel in the rinse bucket and kneeled next to me, grabbing my hand. "We're safe here. I really believe that. Evie knows that. And now with Veronique and Amber, we can't go up there." She motioned over her head to the north.

"I know, I know." I inhaled deeply.

It'd been me, Dad and Becky my whole life. Now she had Evie, and there was Amber and Veronique, all getting used to new lives. Dad and TJ patrolled the island daily with Scott providing help, or whatever else.

And, for a while I had someone of my own.

Wednesday October 26

It happened. As much as I tried to avoid it by simply not going to see him, Mike showed up on the porch and said, "I'm leaving."

"I have to check on my mother. I haven' heard from her or Gil since he left two months ago," he continued. He put his hands in the pockets of his jeans. I'd never seen him in long pants.

"What about the store?" Stupid, stupid thing to say when what I wanted to say was, *what about me?*

He looked at me. My throat tightened. "What about it? What's the point?"

I hoped I was the point. I opened my mouth but knew I'd have trouble speaking.

"When?" I whispered. "How?"

"I need to go soon. Your Dad said he heard there's another storm just rolling off Africa, still over a week away. I'm leaving with the Rayez family."

"Jeff and Sam that stole the soup?" I wanted to shout, angry at myself. I knew this was coming.

"They're just kids. They're scared. We all are."

I started to walk down the front steps. I was shaking. "I'm not."

He reached out and grabbed my hand. His hand was shaking too.

"Yes, you are."

"I can't be. I can't." I kept hold of his hand.

"You have your Dad, Becky, Evie. You have your family."

"We're all family now. What about Pam?"

"I want you to take care of her. You know she won't admit she needs it."

"You knew I wouldn't leave."

"I knew," he said. "But I have to."

I was going to cry, but not in front of him. Not near him. I pulled my hand away, went back in the house, into my home, and shut the door.

When I told Becky the short version, "Mike is leaving," she grabbed me, hugged me, held me and wouldn't let go even when I tried to pull away. Still didn't want to cry. But I did.

I still am.

Friday October 28

No locals' walking parade this year, another Fantasy Fest ritual, and my favorite, a parade of costumed people walking in groups, pairs, individual, all on foot. The route used to pass right by our house. When I was very young I would sit on the porch and watch with my mother. I liked to hand out the colorful, sparkly beads. Dad and TJ always walked, dressed as something—hippies, mimes, Batman and Robin, vampires. After mom left, Dad started taking me with them. My costumes included, Batgirl, Pippi Long-stocking, a zombie, Rosie the riveter. It was always so fun and exhausting. There were drunk people and people in revealing and/or raunchy costumes, but that was Key West, all in fun.

Not this year.

Picked up a signal on the weather radio. It was true, there was another storm but so far away no one could know what would happen at this point. I didn't think hurricane season would ever end. I went back to the list I wrote at the end of May and checked off more of the names. We made it to Tobias. Did we survive this season? I didn't know what I would do when 2016 was over. I didn't have a new calendar. How would I keep track of the days? Down here would it even matter what day it was? What year?

What more is there to say? I don't know what to do from here. There is nothing up there, the mainland, for me. Except Mike. He will be there.

He's leaving tomorrow, early.

I think I'm done. I can't keep this up. Why have I been doing this—writing and writing and writing? For me? For Becky? For Evie, and now Amber? Did I continue, as Becky asked, for people on the mainland, to let them know we are here, and it's okay, for now, we are all okay. And, we might still be here, later.

Or did I do it for him? For Mike.

Either way, I'm done. I have nothing left to say.

I might as well give him this journal. Maybe he can show it to someone. Maybe he will read it. I thought I would have time. I thought he would stay. I thought we would be here, together.

I was wrong.

———

There are no more words, the last pages of the notebook, blank. Seeva closes it, holds it, imagining how such a piece might have travelled so far, so many years ago.

Seeva!

Now Seeva feels Cloyal, strong, for the first time in hours. Feels one's movements—close and quick.

Not alone.

Standing, one sees the dark blue sky out the open door, a royal blue, the sun dropped below the horizon moments ago. Then there is Cloyal and Seeva smiles at the familiar face, the familiar essence, and moves forward. Stops, still holding the notebook. Behind Cloyal stands a human, bearded and very thin, as brown as them. He is back lit, standing in the doorway. But Seeva knows his eyes are blue and bright. Seeva smiles, mimicking Cloyal.

Cloyal speaks.

"Seeva. This is Mike."

He opens his mouth as if to speak and reaches for the notebook. "Mine," his voice cracks. "She gave it to me…Josie. That last night. The night we…"

Seeva holds the notebook out to him.

His hand drops. "I left her," he coughs. "I left her there."

"We know." Seeva and Cloyal say and move toward him, hold his hands, pat his arms. His breath eases.

"We need to go. It's time to leave."

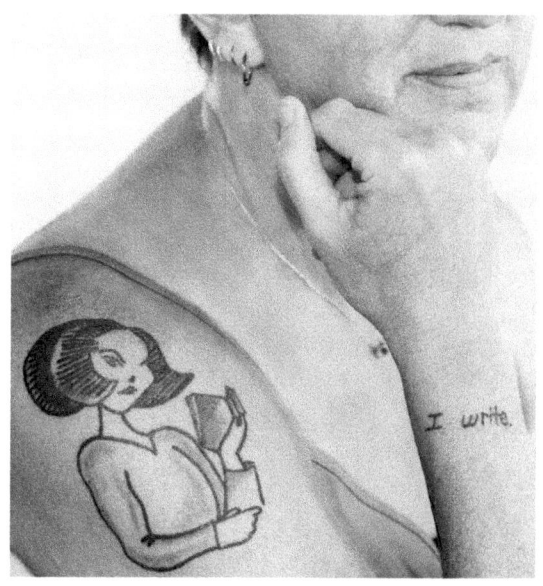

Author Bio

Kristina Neihouse moved to Key West in 1995. She's had a story published in Key West: A collection, won The Studios of Key West 2014 Writes of Spring competition and placed 2nd in the 2018 Tennessee Williams Short Story Contest. In 2016 she was awarded an Anne McKee Artist Fund Grant to publish her first novel Knowing When to Leave.

Kristina is a full-time librarian. When not reading, writing or feeding cats, she participates in 5K runs and triathlons. She spends Saturday nights in the Monroe County Detention Center talking with female inmates about writing and other life choices. Check out www.writeonpublished.wordpress.com to read their work.